OWL and LOST BOY

Praise for Amy Wilson

'This debut is a sparklingly frosty read, full of feisty characters, myth and mystery' *Daily Mail* on *A Girl Called Owl*

'A perfect read for those who love magic and a strong female character proving her place in the world' BookTrust on *A Girl Called Owl*

'Original and compelling . . . an unexpected tale of grief, magic and monsters' Kiran Millwood Hargrave, author of *The Girl of Ink and Stars* on *A Far Away Magic*

'Truly gorgeous magic and a sense of wonder' Stephanie Burgis, author of *The Dragon with the Chocolate Heart* on *A Far Away Magic*

'Literally spellbinding' Piers Torday, author of *The Lost Magician* on *Snowglobe*

'Beautifully written and totally bewitching' Sophie Anderson, author of *The House With Chicken Legs* on *Shadows of Winterspell*

Books by Amy Wilson

A Girl Called Owl

A Far Away Magic

Snowglobe

Shadows of Winterspell

Owl and the Lost Boy

AMY WILSON

OWL
and the
LOST
BOY

Illustrated by
Helen
Crawford-White

MACMILLAN CHILDREN'S BOOKS

Published 2020 by Macmillan Children's Books
an imprint of Pan Macmillan
The Smithson, 6 Briset Street, London EC1M 5NR
Associated companies throughout the world
www.panmacmillan.com

ISBN 978-1-5290-3784-5

1 3 5 7 9 8 6 4 2

A CIP catalogue record for this book is available from the British Library.

Printed and bound by CPI Group (UK) Ltd, Croydon CR0 4YY

For my long-lost father,
Harry Berry Wilson

FABLES & EARTH SPIRITS

F*ew are as powerful in the world of men as the elements who rule the seasons. Spring, summer, autumn and winter; none would happen without them, and often that is the risk, for they fight like warriors to hold their ground.*

The Queen of May is springtime: she comes with all her new life and steps on the coattails of winter, only yielding to summer when that season can no longer be denied. Summer herself, the Lady Midday, must then do battle with the Earl of October, who stalks across the ground, his low song bringing autumn's amber and gold, tucking all things away before Jack Frost, mischievous King of Winter, is released from his world of ice and snow.

Each would rule for years, even longer if they could, and it is only the might of Mother Earth herself that keeps them in order. One cannot happen without the other, and they must each come at their own time. For sure, there are days of summer that burst bright into Jack Frost's wintertime and days of frost that linger long into spring, but those are the exceptions, not the rule.

The rule is Mother Earth's. And the only threat to her order is Father Time himself.

1

Heat presses against my skin, and the closer I get to the small copse of trees the hotter it is. New things have grown here over the summer, glossy vines thick against the ancient trunks of oak and elder, and they reach for me as I move further in. I've tried this so many times since the start of September, and every time I've had to turn back.

I promised myself that this time I'd make it through.

I thrust my hand out against the scented orange flowers and they fight back, jostling against my arm, thick pollen drifting from long yellow stamens. I mutter at them as welts break out on my skin and for a moment the whole world seems to spin. Blue sky, dry grass behind me, the throbbing, malevolent heart of an endless fae summer beating between the trees ahead of me.

I pull back, my chest tightening.

Endless fae summers are not for the faint-hearted. They are certainly not good for *me*, daughter of the King of Winter, Jack Frost. I turn my back on the copse that hides the fae court and look back to the town for a minute, trying to catch my breath. Everything out there is normal: buildings, kids playing in the lengthening shadows, the glow on the horizon as the sun begins to set. Nobody else there knows about the magic that lies beyond these trees. I rub at the sore places on my arms, glaring at the thick new foliage that has beaten me back.

Maybe I should have waited until it was dark. Should have worn gloves. The need to get into the court where all the fae live was so strong and I was so *hot* that I didn't want to wait another moment. I'm tired of this summer. Tired of being alone in it. It's nearly November, for goodness' sake – I want an end to this infernal heat. But as something stirs in the undergrowth, ember-bright and reeking of those vicious orange blooms, I realize with a sinking feeling that I'm just wasting my time. Whatever's going on in there is none of my business. Jack obviously isn't here, and without him there's no place for me.

Trudging home in the blaze of sunset, the air is still warm and thick as syrup in my lungs.

'One day it won't be summer. One day this will be over. Autumn has to come.' I mutter the mantra to myself for the millionth time. Maybe it just feels worse this year because it's the first summer since I met Jack, discovered the fae world and learned about my own wintry powers. Powers that mean precisely nothing in all this fiery heat.

I hesitate when I get to the lane near my flat, seeing the familiar figure of Mallory up ahead, trailing her fingers along the wall as she walks. I see her look up at the flat as she goes past and a little pang goes through me. How did we fall so far apart so quickly? My best friend since the very start of school and now we're barely talking. I didn't try hard enough when she was reeling from her parents' divorce over the holidays.

I was too busy wondering where Jack was, and whether this summer would ever end.

I let my bag drop from my shoulders as I head into the flat, and it falls with a thump on to the floorboards. I take off my shoes and socks for a moment of relief and stomp into the kitchen, making for the fridge. The light isn't working any more, and it's making a loud hoovering sort of noise that doesn't sound healthy, but at least it's cool. Every window in the flat is open and the curtains are half closed to keep out the sun's relentless rays, but it still feels itchy-blanket hot, even as the day fades to dusk.

All summer I waited for autumn. I imagined breathing in knife-sharp cool air. I imagined the leaves on the trees turning to copper and brown. Frost on the rooftops and the crunch of pale, frozen grass beneath my feet. Dancing on the frozen lake, with Jack and the North Wind, spinning fractals across blue ice. Going back to the court and finding welcome there from all the folk I met last winter: the Lady of the Lake, the Green Man and all the tiny flitting fairies.

But it hasn't happened. Daybreak is still like molten fire and it sticks to everything. Pavements are scorching, rivers are dust, the fields that should be freezing now are tinder-dry and the court seems to be out of bounds. At night, my dreams are full of ice and adventure, and, when I wake, for a moment my whole room is alight with their remnants. Ice covers every surface, frost runs up the walls in spirals and icicles clink at the bottom of the curtains. Then the sky begins to brighten, and the winter wonderland I've made in my sleep melts, and I am exhausted at the start of another day of this cursed summer.

Grabbing a glass of water, I head for my room, swishing the curtains as I pass to make a draught. The rug makes my feet itch and I can hardly bear to look at the bed.

'Owl!' Mum calls, clattering down the steps from her studio and following me in. Her dark hair is piled on top of her head and she's barefoot, her arms glistening with sweat. There are sweeps of charcoal across her cheeks. 'How was your day?'

'Hot,' I say.

She looks me up and down.

'Cold shower, then?'

'Yes.'

'You look tired,' she says. 'Did you see Mallory today?'

'Not to speak to.' I sigh, and she presses her lips into a sad smile. She misses her too.

'What about Alberic?'

Mum's had a soft spot for Alberic ever since I brought him home with me last year. He's the son of the treacherous Earl of October, ruler of autumn, and therefore about as normal as I am. His human mother died when he was small, so he lives in the court with his fae family and only ventured into the human world for the first time last year, when he started going to my school. He was the one who first showed me Jack, showed me where I came from. We watched him playfight with Boreas, the North Wind, and he warned me how devious the fae could be. Now he's missing. They're all missing, and so is autumn. And I can't even get in there to find out what's going on. As soon as summer started, the path got choked with those horrible flowers. It felt like rejection and it hurt, but Jack had warned me that summer was the time for me to rest, and I guessed that was just how he always felt in summer: locked out. Only now it's gone on way too long.

'No sign,' I say now, collapsing on to the bed.

Mum frowns and flumps down on to the bed with me. 'Perhaps Jack might know?'

'I don't know where he is *either*!' I say. 'And he's not likely to be here any time soon with all this stupid heat we're having.'

'It is a worry,' she says, picking at a loose strand of the quilt she made for me years ago. 'There's lots of talk about it out there.' She looks at me, and bounces off the bed, pulling me up after her. 'Food. I'll make dinner, you have a shower – one step at a time, we'll get there.'

She reaches out and puts her arms around me, and I let my head fall on her shoulder, just for a moment, even though it's too warm and we're both sweaty and it's a bit gross.

'OK?' she says, as she moves away.

'Fine.' I nod, and head for the bathroom.

I think I'd live in the shower if I could. The water is cold, and by the time I finish there's a little shiver of ice in the air. Not much, but enough for me to breathe deeply without feeling like I'm being smothered. My mind clears, and when I join Mum in our little sitting room I spy her old book of fae legends on the crowded shelves, its spine glinting gold in the dappled sunlight, and with a rush of excitement I realize I know just what to do.

I spend the rest of the evening watching nature documentaries with Mum while she sketches, waiting for her to leave the room so I can check out the book: *Fablef and Earth-Fpiritf: How to Meet Them and How to Find Your Way to Your Own Fpirit Felf.* Mum was the one who passed the book to me last winter, when I was just discovering the fae world and how to use the wintry powers I'd inherited from Jack. It's full of stories about fae legends – the Green Man, the North Wind, the Queen of the May – and I went on to meet most of them, which Mum knows. But since my adventures last winter she's been a bit more guarded. I am not allowed to the court on my own, and I can't get in anyway. She hasn't forbidden the book, but that's just because she hasn't thought of it yet. To be honest, I hadn't thought of it until I spotted it today. There's an incantation in there, which just might help, if I can get to it. We're on our third dose of sea-life rescues when eventually she goes upstairs to the attic to get more charcoal, and I manage to get the book to my room without her noticing.

But when I return to it later, the windows full open to let in as much of the night breeze as possible, there's something wrong. The ancient browned pages that were filled with legends and stories – of Jack and the North Wind, and of their other worlds – are blank. I flick through in a flurry, getting more and more anxious as I go. This was my fall-back plan. This was supposed to give me answers, but it's just like the court, completely unavailable. No fae magic for Owl.

This can't be right. Late October, and still locked out when we should be in full autumn, with Jack bringing the first frosts. I close my eyes and breathe slowly, but the hits keep coming. No court. No Mallory, no Alberic and no Jack. No incantation. I stare around at the sketches of owls on my walls and blink at them, wondering for a dizzy second if I just imagined everything last winter, when my powers emerged as frost on my skin.

No. It was real – and I'm just going to have to keep going. Something's gone drastically wrong with the fae world, and somehow both Alberic and Jack are caught up in it. I fall into the sheets and reach out to the wooden owl on my bedpost. Mother Earth appeared as an owl last winter and I've often wondered if she uses owls to keep an eye on what's going on.

'What's going on?' I ask, my fingers tracing the familiar rough texture of the wooden feathers. The owl snaps its eyelids, and I draw back with a thrill in my belly. I definitely didn't imagine *that*.

Magic is still here, somewhere.

I stare the owl in the eye, and give it a long, cool look, imagining I really am talking to Mother Earth. 'I know you don't like to get involved, but summer is going on forever, Jack's nowhere to be seen and Alberic is missing. Someone needs to do *something* – don't they? I've tried to get in there to check, but it's too hot, and even the book is empty . . .'

But all that comes back is a thick, warm silence. Naturally. Even if this is some sort of fae emergency, Mother Earth is not the sort to interfere. I'm just lying here talking to furniture. I stretch out, trying to find the cool places in my bed, and drift into a restless sleep, dreaming of my adventures with Jack last winter, that feeling of ice on my skin, through my hair, spilling from my footsteps.

LADY MIDDAY

What is the world of summer? It is to drowse in the midday sun under a cobalt-blue sky. It is golden fields and dandelion wishes carried on the merest breath of wind. The heat of that place is a blanket that steals over you, at first welcome, and later stifling.

Beware the summer; beware the Lady Midday. She has no mercy. She rules her world with a fiery whip and the unspent thunder of a hundred days without rain. Her sprites are flame-bright and their footprints smoulder in their wake. There are golden cities in the world of summer, flashing towers and fiery lakes and pale, shifting deserts beneath star-filled skies.

The storms, when they come, are a sky-crash of light, and when the rain falls it is a flood of warm tears. They shake the very foundations of Lady Midday's world of summer and make her rage.

She does not love humanity, but she loves to bask in her earthly season and she hungers for it — stealing in as early as March, and lingering well into September. At their most potent her days are still and heavy; they will steal hours, make the smallest of tasks feel mountainous. The Lady makes her way through them slowly, languorous, her golden cloak turning the ground to dust.

Beware the Lady Midday. She is fickle as the summer storm; she is at her most dangerous when her gentle song resounds.

2

The morning brings a fresh wave of heat. Mum is distracted, preparing for a new art course at the university, and seems to have lost every pencil, sketchpad and paintbox she ever owned. I gulp down orange juice while she flashes around the flat, humming an angry little song about all the lost things. She thrusts a banana at me as I head out the door.

'Most important meal of the day!' she says.

'A banana?'

'Breakfast.'

'It's too hot for breakfast.'

'I knew you'd say that, hence the banana.' She nods. 'Did you put your lunch in your bag?'

'Yes, thank you.'

'I put an ice pack in,' she says proudly. 'Found it in

the freezer yesterday, lurking behind some old fish.'

'Lovely,' I say. 'You have a pencil behind your ear, you know. And one in your hair. Are they the ones you're looking for?'

She puts her fingers up and pulls them out, rolling her eyes. 'That's some of them anyway. Thank you, Owl. Now, have a good day.' She gives me a hug, and watches me down the communal steps, until I flap at her to go back inside.

'It's cool!' she shouts.

'No, it's really not!' I shout back.

She grins, and closes the door.

School is a nightmare. The fans in the classrooms just circulate hot air, and the teachers are cranky. History is sweltering and Miss Leonard has a tongue like a viper; any sign of inattention and she lashes out. The Women of the World are deserving of our attention and she's determined to make sure they get it.

The problem is that I can hardly keep my eyes open. Time after time they drift closed, and I wake with a jolt. Humidity fills my lungs, my brain, and my skin feels like it's on fire. Flashes of yesterday's futile fight through the branches of the summer court keep on coming.

'Owl?'

'Yes!' I sit bolt upright.

'Are you all right? You look very drowsy.'

'It's hot,' I manage.

Miss Leonard frowns. 'Nobody can deny that. Do you need some air?'

'*Is* there any?' I ask, and Fergus snorts next to me.

'Very droll,' Miss Leonard says. 'Why don't you go to student reception and get some iced water? You're rather distracting everybody else.'

'Sorry,' I say, sliding out of my desk, gathering my things and dragging my bag along behind me. Someone laughs, and I'm pretty sure it's at me, but I don't look back.

The corridors are shiny, bright and endless. I trail one hand along the wall for a moment of cool, and so that I don't fall over. Student reception is on the other side of the school, and the further I go, the more I start to feel like I'm hardly here at all. An endless, brutal summer is no good at all for anyone, and it's torture for someone who literally has winter in their genetic make-up.

'Shall we call your parents?' the receptionist asks, looking me up and down when I get there on wobbly legs, my head pounding. Immediately I get an image of Jack Frost striding through the corridors, ice in his wake, silver eyes flashing. Not that you can call the King of Winter on a phone. Or that he'd come anyway. Mum would, but then she'd worry.

'Ah no, thank you,' I say. 'I'll be fine in a moment.'

'Are you sure?' she asks, coming closer and propelling me into one of the woolly chairs. My skin shrieks as the fibres cling to my legs, but I force myself to sit still. 'You look rather fae.'

'Pardon?' I ask, squinting up at her. Did she really say that? I can't make out her features – the air is too hot, too bright.

'You look a little faint,' she says, handing me a cup of water. 'Here, have this and rest a moment.'

Faint, I repeat in my head, laughing at myself. Not *fae*. Though I am fae. Half fae, anyway. Just like Alberic, with his fae elemental father. What if he's just off with the rest of them somewhere? What if they're in their own worlds, watching from afar, laughing at the silly little human who is trying with all her might to get in?

'*That's not it,*' a dry, crackling sort of voice whispers in my ear. I look around. There's nobody here but the receptionist, who's busy at her computer. I'm delirious, obviously. Or – is it Mother Earth, coming to help me after my plea last night?

'It might be,' I whisper, just in case. 'And they'll come back soon and everything will be better.'

'*Who's going to make them come back, though?*' the voice asks. '*If you don't?*'

'Oh, someone better than me,' I say, closing my eyes to see the forest Alberic and I walked through last winter in Jack's own frozen world. Black silhouettes of trees, the crunch of snow beneath our feet and an owl, who swoops through the forest towards me. 'Y'know. Someone stronger, wiser . . .'

The owl hangs before me, its golden eyes staring.

'You,' it says.

'Owl?'

I open my eyes, and Mallory is there.

'Are you OK? Someone said you'd been sent here . . .'

'I'm good,' I say. I pick up my bag and stand, and the room sways – only a little bit, but of course Mallory never misses anything.

'What's going on?' she whispers, grabbing me by the arm before I topple back into the chair, looking me up and down. 'What's happened to your arms?'

I look down. They're still red and swollen from my

brush with the new summer plants last night.

'Nothing! Don't worry about it.' I straighten myself and pull my bag on to my shoulder, moving away from her.

'Of course I'm going to worry about it. I'm your—'

'My what, Mallory?' I demand, suddenly flaring. 'My friend? I thought we were past that.'

'Well, we're not,' she says, sticking her chin out. 'Even if you've been avoiding me.'

'Avoiding you! *You've* been avoiding *me!*'

'Girls?' the receptionist interrupts, frowning. 'I don't think this is what the doctor ordered!'

'No, sorry,' Mallory says, while I stand there gasping like a fish out of water. 'I was saying I'd walk her home and she's being stubborn.'

'I'd let your friend walk you home if I were you,' the receptionist says. 'Either that or I'll be calling your parents to come and get you.'

'My mum, you mean,' I say. 'I don't have *parents*. Not everybody gets two *parents*.'

'I can't say I recommend two parents actually,' Mallory says, giving the receptionist one of her gleaming smiles as she carts me away down the corridor. 'Two parents are just hard work,' she huffs. 'Anyway, what about Jack?'

'Jack doesn't count,' I say. 'Doesn't w̶ father, never was a father, now I don't even know w̶ he is. I haven't seen him since March!'

'Were you expecting summer picnics with him?' Mallory asks.

'What if I was?' I say. 'Bet you had a summer picnic with your dad!'

'OK,' she says. 'Let's stop. I'm sorry. I'm sorry you miss him.'

'I don't miss him – he's a pain,' I say. 'I'm sorry you miss yours.'

'Well,' she says. 'It's going to be all right.' She keeps one hand behind me as we head down the steps and out of school, and though she doesn't touch me, I can tell she's ready, just in case I stumble.

'Why don't we talk any more?' I ask as we head out into the furnace of mid-afternoon. My knees are like jelly, and I feel a bit like crying, just because she's being nice to me. I've missed her so much. The heat rises off the pavement, eating into the soles of my shoes. 'I can't . . . It's too HOT!'

'Give me your bag,' she says, hauling it off me and pulling me out of the way of a group of boys heading for the bus stop. 'Now take your tie off . . .' She takes that too, and then she gets her water bottle out of her bag, and upends it all over my head.

'Mallory!' I gasp.

She has her lips pursed, as if she's trying not to laugh. 'Do you feel cooler?'

'Yes,' I say, plucking at the front of my shirt.

'What did happen to your arms, anyway?' she asks, frowning.

'I tried to get into the court, and there's all this new stuff grown up around the entrance . . . I must be allergic to it. Jack told me that summer was a time of rest – I didn't realize he meant I'd literally get locked out of the fae world.'

I sigh, and she propels me out of the gate and towards home. We don't talk a lot more, because I can't, and she's busy making sure I'm walking in a straight line. By the time we reach my front door I'm sure there's steam coming out of my nose.

'Shall I come in for a minute?'

'Sure,' I say, fiddling with the key, finally managing to get the door open. I trudge up the stairs and into the flat with her close on my heels. The curtains are all drawn and the fridge is making its usual racket, but it feels calm after the blaze of outside. I perch on the edge of the kitchen table and breathe it in. Mallory drops our bags and makes herself at home, getting glasses and ice. It tinkles as she comes towards me.

'Thank you,' I say, looking her in the eye so she knows I mean it.

'You look terrible,' she says.

I shake my head and drop into one of the kitchen chairs.

'I don't say it to be mean!' she says, sitting next to me. 'Are you sick?'

'No,' I say. 'I mean, not in any of the usual ways. Summer was hard . . . and it just keeps coming. The longer it goes on the worse I feel, and I thought it was just because of who I am but now I'm worried about it. Summer just shouldn't be going on this long, and maybe something's really wrong but I can't get into the court, and I don't know where Alberic is, or Jack – and the book of fablef isn't working . . .'

'Slow down,' she says. 'Tell me everything.'

'But Mallory . . .'

She looks at me.

'Do you really want to know? Don't you have enough going on right now?'

I know her parents' separation has been really hard

on her. Everything changed when her dad moved out, and then it just kept changing. Over the summer it became official: they were getting a divorce. Only I didn't know that until school went back, because she'd stopped answering my texts, and when I went to her house to see her one day, she wasn't there. She had separate holidays, with her mum and then her dad, and it was probably completely weird. I wanted to talk to her about it, but by the time we caught up everything felt different between us as well.

'I was angry,' she says. 'I still am, sometimes. But right now I'm worried about Alberic. And you. So can we focus on that?'

'. . . and now I know it's up to me, so there's no time to waste, Mallory. Alberic's been missing since school started back.' I pause to take a breath and look across at Mallory, who has been listening patiently.

'Do you think Alberic's in the court?' she asks. 'I tried looking myself as soon as I realized he hadn't come back – I got into the copse of trees but it was really overgrown, and I never found the lake, or the rest of the court. I thought it was just hidden to my human eyes.'

'You got further than I did. Maybe in the summer

Lady Midday uses it as her own court, with her own rules, I don't know. It's so hot in that little copse now, and there are things creeping in the undergrowth. I think they're her little fae embers – surely they shouldn't still be there, now? Am I losing it, Mallory? This isn't normal, is it – all this heat?'

'No,' she says, looking out of the window. 'I mean, I don't think I feel it as badly as you, but it's definitely not normal. Maybe we should try the court again, together.'

I stare at her. She stares at me.

'You really want to?'

'Alberic's missing,' she says with a shrug. 'And summer is going on too long. Alberic is the son of autumn, so those two things have to be connected, don't they? So yes I want to. I think we have to, Owl.'

'OK,' I say. 'Tomorrow then. If you're sure.'

'I'm sure,' she says.

And it isn't exactly business as usual, there are still funny spaces in our conversation, and sharp edges in our words, but now Mallory is on the case everything does feel more manageable.

3

'Sure you're ready for this?' Mallory asks with a frown the next day.

'Yes,' I say. 'Only I can't . . .' My heart hammers as I turn from her to face the copse, where I was welcome last winter. Where I cannot go now. Heat oozes through the undergrowth, and my ears are ringing. I put my hands on my knees, close my eyes and try to bolster myself. If I don't do this now, I'll go home and regret it all night, worry about Alberic, worry that I could've done more if I'd just tried harder. What if I've left it too late and something really is wrong? I should've tried harder to keep in touch with him. He helped me to understand, last winter, and his life wasn't easy then. We're both half human and half fae, only I grew up with my human mother in the human world, and he grew up here with the Earl of October, who hates everything human, including that part of his son.

'Owl?' Mallory's hand is cool on my back, and the grass beneath my feet blurs as hot tears swell in my eyes. I blink hard, and pull myself up.

'I'm fine,' I say. 'Let's go.'

'Let me go first,' she says, pulling me behind her.

'Mallory!'

'You're allergic to something here, Owl, remember? Let me go first . . . and pull your sleeves down.'

I open my mouth to protest, and shut it again. A little squiggle of hope thrills in my chest as she reaches back her hand and grabs mine.

'What is all this stuff anyway,' she mutters, charging at it, pushing it away with her free hand. 'It wasn't here before.'

'Or you couldn't *see* it before, with your human eyes. Now you're with me, perhaps that changes things. It's all the doing of Lady Midday.' I whisper it, because Lady Midday is the fearsome fae ruler of summer and I can feel she's close; there's a malevolence to the heat that is definitely fae-like. 'She must be keeping autumn away somehow.'

Mallory hesitates, grimacing. 'You mean the Earl?'

I nod, though she can't see me. She's marching now, dragging me behind her as the way gets wider and wilder. The Earl of October is the elemental ruler of autumn, and he's the one who schemed with the Queen of May to banish Jack Frost last year. The seasons always battle for their place in the year, but as we get closer towards the fae court it feels like this one is a battle already won by Lady Midday. Heat blooms here, and though it's darker under the canopy of trees there's no relief. The air is close and damp, and a low mist clings to our ankles.

'OK?' Mallory looks back. 'You're very pale.'

'Just hot,' I manage. I pull away from her and turn in the clearing. We should already be there, but it all feels unfamiliar. 'We're getting there, Mallory. I can feel it. Where's the lake?'

'That's what I couldn't find when I tried before.' She frowns. 'Can't you feel it?' She wiggles her fingers in a magical way and I stare at her. 'The magic, I mean!'

I peer up into the branches of the trees, looking for some sign of life. The whole place is still, suffocating. Last time I was here was the end of winter, and it had become like a second home. Tiny winged fairies knew me well enough not to attack when I visited, and the sprites would flick leaves at me. There's nothing now, except the occasional glimmer of those fiery figures that I glimpsed before. Everything else has been driven out by Lady Midday – they must have been.

'Oh come on,' I mutter. 'This is stupid – you must all be here somewhere!'

An emerald-green bird darts out of the branches next to us and flits down a darkened, bramble-strewn path. Mallory and I look at each other.

'It could be a sign,' she says doubtfully. 'Come on. Let's go.'

'Alberic's not going to be here, Mallory,' I say. 'Nor is Jack. It's too hot.'

'We're not going back now,' she hisses, wrestling her way through dry branches and tangled vines. I step after her, wincing as they wind over my skin.

'If any of them were here, they'd have come to see us.'

'What if they're all locked in somehow?' She looks back and frowns, wrapping her sleeves over her hands before releasing me from the bright green clawed trails. 'These things *really* don't like you.'

'I'm the enemy,' I say with a growl at the back of my throat.

'Well, can't you fight back, then?' she asks, picking a thorned vine away from my knees. 'Use your wintry powers to freeze them!'

'They're not working.'

She pauses and stares at me. 'Of course,' she says, her eyes widening. 'Because it's summer . . .' She looks around as the undergrowth writhes. 'This *may* have been a bad idea.'

'That's what I've been telling myself all summer,' I say. 'But it'll be November soon, and I can't keep walking away. If Alberic *is* missing, maybe the Earl is missing too, and that'll be why it's still summer – no autumn!'

'Right,' she says, turning back to the path. 'I just wish I'd brought a knife, then. Or, I mean, have you *tried* using your powers in here, to fight all this off?'

'Not since spring,' I say. 'The last time I got this far was when summer was just starting, before I went away with Mum. I got through the outer edge of the trees, but when I tried to go further in towards the court something pushed back against me. Jack had warned me that summer would be difficult, so I thought it was because of the whole winter thing, and I left.'

'*I'm* here this time,' Mallory says. 'If you want to try.

If you want to carry on . . .'

'I'll try,' I say after a moment. I close my eyes, and reach into myself. In winter, using frost is easy – too easy. My skin is covered in an instant, and it spreads easy as breathing. Last winter I froze Mallory's bedroom. I made sparkling chandeliers, and ice rinks out of lakes. But right now, in this heat, it's hard to even imagine the bright silver of that other winter world. A flicker of something rushes through me as I remember. It twists and blooms with the beat of my heart. I draw away from Mallory and start to move forward, my eyes still closed. Frost sweeps over my skin and the vines whisper, but I thrust out my cold hands, and they move away, hissing.

'It's working,' whispers Mallory.

My heart is loud in my head. I feel hotter than ever on the inside, but my skin is still cool, so I keep moving, until I feel the way open out before me.

We burst into the clearing of the fae court, and I stumble, heat crashing over me, a wave of darkness that takes my knees out. I sit hard on the ground, and Mallory hauls me over to sit against a tree – she's saying something I can't hear.

Help, I whisper in my mind as she moves away from

me. *JACK, WHERE ARE YOU?*

Of course there's no answer. I hadn't exactly expected Jack to be here, in the middle of all this, but we're right in the heart of the court now and nothing is stirring. The Green Man is silent and still on the edge of the lake, and the air is thick with the scent of those large orange blooms. Where *is* everybody? Where's the Lady of the Lake? Where are the silver-winged fairies, and the tiny sprites? Why does the Green Man slumber through my call? The clearing that was covered in tiny flowers and tangled wood at the start of spring is darker now. New plants with thick green leaves bustle up against the slender birch trunks and make islands in the lake. The ivy has wilted, and the lush vines have swarmed through everything. The lake itself is low and brown, and mirror-still.

And Mallory is on her knees, staring into it.

I push myself up, breath tearing through my chest, and stagger over to her.

'Mall?'

She doesn't answer, leaning in closer.

'What is it?' I pull at her and she starts.

'What?'

'What were you staring at?'

'I thought I saw Alberic. But it got misty, and then I saw stars and mountains and cities, but they were all falling . . .' She shakes her head, pulling herself up. 'I don't know what it was.'

'Was Alberic in the mountains?'

'No. He was in darkness.' She shivers. 'He was lost. Someone here must know what's going on. Where are you all *hiding*? Where's ALBERIC?'

'They're not here, Mallory,' I whisper. 'We should go . . .'

'Oh but not so soon. Who were you expecting?' comes a voice that resonates with thunder. I've only heard about her from my mother's old book of fae, but she's instantly recognizable: Lady Midday, the mistress of summer, is here. Her song is lulling soft and fierce beneath and she sweeps towards us, a heat haze rippling the air around her. Her cloak billows behind her and the grass it touches turns brown. It makes my eyes hurt to look at her; she is amber and golden and she blazes with all the strength of noon.

'Now,' she says, staring between us. 'What are you doing here? This is my place.'

'Is it?' I ask. I've never known such stillness here. It's eerie. I gesture at the great oak that is the Green

33

Man, unstirring and silent. Last time I was here the trees were full of tiny lightning-winged fairies, and the watchful eyes of stoats and weasels, bright green frogs and darting songbirds. Now the only creatures moving are the ones that keep close to her cloak. Golden-skinned goblins, and sprites with flaming hair, all of them watching us in silence. 'I thought it was Mother Earth's court – it was last winter. What have you done to them all?'

'Oh summer is long, and summer is drowsy. They do not suffer. You are impertinent to challenge me thus in my own season.' She frowns. 'I smell winter on you. What is that?' She tilts her head and glares down at me. 'Ah!' she says. 'Now I have it. You are the Owl I've heard of. Jokul's daughter!'

'Yes,' I say, wishing I had better words. Or any words at all. I can't think straight when she's staring at me. Fortunately, it takes a lot more to make Mallory tongue-tied.

'Do you really think you can make it summer all year round?' Mallory asks, startling the Lady. 'Drought kills things – you do know that?'

'What business is this of yours, little human?'

'Isn't it everybody's business? The world, I mean?'

'The world!' The Lady laughs and clouds shift in the skies above us as static rolls through the clearing. 'The world has been left to humanity's care for too long – and what good has that done? Humans kill things too, you know.'

'But it can't just be summer forever!' I say. 'Every-where?'

'Without autumn – and *I* don't know what happened to that ridiculous Earl – who is to stop me? You?' She laughs, and static crackles in the air between us. 'Can you do your frosting in the midst of all this?' She sweeps her arm out, and heat flares around her, making the air warp. The fire sprites clamber to her shoulders, watching us intently with coal-bright eyes. It's hard to breathe, hard to stay standing before her. Mallory shifts closer to my side. 'Of course you can't,' the Lady says. 'And neither can your father, just in case you were wondering . . .'

'Where *is* Jack?' I demand. 'And where's Alberic? What have you done with everybody?'

'Have you lost all your friends?' She smiles. 'They have abandoned you, child. Perhaps you should stay away yourself. I'm supposing the heat isn't very good for your health, being your father's daughter . . .'

'We'll find them,' I say with a growl in my voice, 'and then we'll be back. This isn't going to last forever!'

'Who knows,' she says smoothly, scooping up one of the sprites and cradling it in her hands. 'I didn't ask for this, you know. I was expecting Sorbus to come with that ridiculous autumnal racket, and make the world a duller place but he didn't, and neither did his son. I don't know where they've gone and I didn't make the others go. All I have done is stepped into the breach, my dear.'

'Stepped into the breach?'

'There must be a season!' she snaps. 'If it shall not be autumn, then it shall be summer, for winter cannot come until autumn is done.' She leans in towards me. 'You know that much, little Owl, do you not? But you do look so weak and hot – let me give you a little refreshment . . . and a warning. Stay away, my dear. Forget this elemental streak of yours – it does you no good. You are not strong enough to mean anything here. Go home, and be human.'

She raises her arms and lightning forks over the lake as the skies rumble and split, bringing a sudden downpour of rain. The Lady is untouched by it and turns her back, the cloak rustling as she heads deeper into the woods, repeating her warning as she goes. Mallory and I are quickly soaked.

'Come on.' Mallory pulls at me.

But I don't want to move. The rain is cool against my skin; the sound of it falling into the lake is like music. And the Lady's words are still chiming against my insides, making everything hurt. *Be human.* As if it were a small thing and the other part of me meant nothing at all. As if Jack meant nothing at all.

'We should go,' Mallory says. 'Really. Before she comes back.'

I lift my face to the sky and stick my tongue out to catch the rain. It doesn't linger long on my skin, and the air is still hot – perhaps it's only a trick. 'This is our chance to look though, Mallory. Once we leave here, we may not be able to get back again – you heard her warning.'

'She was just being mean. What are we going to look for?' Mallory asks, scanning the clearing. The colours are vivid in the rain: bright greens, and the orange and pink of the summer blooms. 'We already have, Owl.'

'She might have got rid of the fae, somehow,' I say. 'But she can't have got rid of everything. Alberic lived here, Mallory. He's half human – he must've had a home. We should find it, while we're here, and look for clues . . .'

Her eyes light up. 'That's a great idea!'

'Can't believe I never looked for it before.' I frown. 'What kind of friend doesn't know where a person lives, Mallory?'

'He was secretive, Owl. Let's not feel guilty right now – let's get on and find it. It would be around here somewhere, wouldn't it?'

'I think so. The Green Man and the Lady of the Lake are the ones who look out for him – it would make sense that he lives with them.' I squint up at the Green Man. 'I guess we could climb – we'd get a good view from up there, wouldn't we.'

Mallory hesitates, and I remember that she doesn't like heights – she was never one for climbing frames. We went to a party at one of those outdoor jungle places once, and she spent the whole time helping to organize sandwiches, but I wasn't fooled.

'You don't have to!' I say.

'Yes, I do,' she says. 'We're in this together, remember?'

'I do,' I say. 'Come on, then . . .'

I put a foot against the creviced bark and grab for

the lowest branch, hauling myself up. The Green Man rumbles, but it quickly turns to a snore.

'OK?' I ask, peering down from a branch. Mallory's got one foot on the trunk, one on the dry ground. 'You really don't have to . . . I'm just going to have a look.'

'I'm coming,' says Mallory. 'It might just take me a bit longer – you've got very nimble, being fae and all.'

I think of my evening forays with Jack. Skating on black ice, leaping up buildings, dusting them with frost, reaching for the hands of the clock in the clocktower at the centre of town and watching as icicles gleamed under the moon.

It feels like a long time ago.

'Half fae,' I say, reaching for the next branch. Higher, and higher I climb, hearing Mallory's movements behind me, and a fair bit of swearing, to be honest.

'Do you need a hand?' I call down at one point, when there's a scuffling sound and a little yelp below me.

'I'm FINE,' she bellows. 'Can you see anything yet?'

I pull back a bunch of leaves, hauling myself on to the next branch. 'Mostly leaves . . .'

And then everything changes.

The Green Man is no ordinary tree. We know this. Anything is possible in the world of fae, but this is really like a dream. I must be more than halfway up the main trunk by now, and suddenly the network of branches has spread to cradle a small treehouse built of old wood and curving to fit within the thick canopy. The roof is steeply pitched, and covered in old leaves, and wooden shutters cover the windows. I haul myself up on to the narrow wooden ledge that runs all around it and pick my way through vines of ivy to a small, round door.

'Owl?'

'Keep coming!' I say. 'We've found it, Mallory! Step on to the ledge, and keep coming round . . . Can you make it?'

'Right behind you,' says Mallory, edging into sight. She looks a bit flustered.

'Come on.' I haul at her arm and we clatter at the door together, relieved when it yields. Alberic's always been really private about his life, and last winter he actively tried to keep me away from it; I wonder how he'd feel now, knowing that we're in his home. I only wish I'd done it sooner. He's my friend – he's been to my house – we've spent time together, at school and with the fae. I let him keep me at arm's length, let Jack convince me I didn't really belong here in summer. Now I wish I hadn't. I look at Mallory. I've been so caught up in what's happening to me – what kind of friend have I been?

'It's very dark,' Mallory whispers after a moment. We're standing on the inside of the treehouse and light filters through the cracks in the wood, making bars of mist. I tread over to one of the window shutters and push it open. The pale light of the moon filters in through the fine strands of cobwebs that stretch across the ceiling and into dark corners.

'Wow,' says Mallory.

4

The floor is carpeted with oak and sycamore leaves in shades of green, gold and amber. A narrow wood-framed bed has been built into the far corner, rumpled blankets trailing to the floor. Schoolbooks are piled haphazardly on to a chair by the bed, and Alberic's uniform hangs from a small silver hook on the wall. There's a little table by the open window, with a couple of tin mugs stacked on top of a plate and bowl. It's all clean and orderly – a single battered cooking pot, a tarnished copper ladle and a jug hang from little hooks on the side of the table, and a thin towel is neatly folded on the single stool. All of it is covered in a fine layer of dust. He hasn't been here for weeks.

'Where does he cook?' Mallory whispers. 'Do you think he eats here on his own, Owl?' She prowls over to the bed and knocks into an old lamp hanging from the ceiling, sending dust spiralling to the floor. It glitters as it falls and she looks back at me, but neither of us says anything.

I don't know what to say.

It's beautiful, and perfect. Everything in order and all a person needs. Except, not really. I think of my room and all the things in it, most of which I don't even notice any more, and feel a flush run through me.

'Where's all his stuff?' I whisper.

Mallory turns to me from the bed with a worn teddy in her hand.

'Oh,' I manage. She turns back and tucks it carefully into the blankets. 'It isn't much, is it?'

'Well,' she says, sitting on the edge of the bed, running one finger over the schoolbooks. More dust. 'Where is he, then? He hasn't been here for a few weeks, Owl.'

I sweep my fingertips over the rough walls. I don't even know what we're looking for.

'Check under the bed?' I manage. 'Maybe he has a secret tin of . . . secrets?'

'That would be convenient,' she says. She peers under the bed, and sighs. 'Nothing.'

The light coming through the window takes on a golden hue and I snap the shutter closed.

'Lady Midday's coming back!'

'What do we do?'

'We can't get stuck here all night – we'll have to make a run for it,' I say, and we rush out of the treehouse, sliding down the Green Man's branches and dropping to the ground. Racing through the clearing, we fight back the reaching, stinging vines as the golden light grows.

The ground is still damp beneath our feet as we trample back through the undergrowth, but as we head out on to the old school field it's clear that it didn't rain here. The earth is still parched, pale and cracked beneath the streetlights, the grass in scrubby, worn-out patches.

'I guess it was a local storm,' I say, panting. 'We need to find him, Mallory.'

'And the Earl.'

I sigh, trying to catch my breath. He's not my favourite person. He was at the root of all the trouble we had last year, when I first discovered Jack Frost was my father, and he's meaner than most, even when he's not plotting against everybody else.

'Do you think they're somewhere together?' I can hear the doubt in my own voice. I can't picture them on a trip together; the Earl was furious after Alberic stood up to him last winter.

Why didn't I worry about it before?

'We should've checked in on Alberic over the summer,' Mallory says in a glum voice.

'I know,' I say. 'But you had a lot going on, Mallory. We can't change it now. We just need to find him.'

She nods, but her face is bleak, and that tension is back between us. So much has happened and I guess that no matter how long you've known somebody, there's always new stuff that can change everything.

'Do you want to talk about it?' I ask.

'About what? Alberic?'

'No. Well. We should talk about him – I should've tried harder before. It's been bothering me. I meant your parents.'

'Oh.' She scuffs her feet on the rough ground as we head towards home. 'Well. They're OK. And it's kind of nice having two bedrooms, I suppose.'

'What's your dad's place like?'

'It's all right. He says it's temporary, while they sort things out with money and stuff, so there's no point getting too settled. My room's all right, although he went out and got lots of girly things to make it feel like home, even though it's temporary.' She shakes her head, but she's smiling. 'The duvet cover has actual ruffles!'

'I quite like a ruffle,' I say.

'Owl, you do not. Imagine if you got home and your mum had got a load of flowery pink things in and a heart-shaped mirror with sparkles in the frame. And an enormous stuffed unicorn.'

'A *unicorn*?'

'With a rainbow mane, and a long flowing tail.'

'You like it, right?'

'I've called it Eugene.' She nods. 'And it's all very tragic, but he was so nervous and excited about it when he showed me . . .'

'He's trying, isn't he? Wish Jack'd get me a unicorn.'

'You don't! And, besides, he's given you actual powers.'

'Actual powers that could do with a bit of fixing.'

'Has it been this bad all summer?' she asks as we traipse up the lane. The moon is bright and full, and the narrow pavement is thick with shadows.

I shiver, despite the warmth of the evening. 'It feels

like the summer's stuck on my skin. Like another layer, suffocating and itchy.'

'And your frost is underneath? What about Jack?'

'I'd imagine it would be tough on him too – if he was here.'

There's a long silence.

'I'm sorry . . .'

I shrug. 'Nothing to say, is there? He's Jack Frost. He wasn't going to be setting up home and making a room for me.'

'Have you tried to go to his world? I mean, he has a home there. You could spend time with him that way?'

'No,' I say. 'The book isn't working and I don't know how to get there without it. Even if I did . . .' I don't know how to explain it to her. I wanted him to come to me, to make an effort. I don't want to be chasing after him, asking for something he probably can't even give. 'He doesn't want me there.'

'He told you that?' Her voice rises with indignation.

'Pretty much.' I wince, remembering the way that conversation went, the last time I saw him. I was so angry that I can hardly remember it straight. I *do* remember walking away from him, knowing it would be months before I'd see him again and hardly caring.

'Oh,' Mallory says, apparently lost for words for the first time ever. 'I'm sure he didn't really mean it . . .'

I shrug. 'Felt like it at the time.'

'That's rubbish. I'm sorry, Owl.'

'Me too. I should've talked to you about it before. Do you want to come in?' I ask as we get to my flat.

'I'd better get home – Mum's got a homework schedule.'

'A schedule?'

'With rewards and everything.'

'You are being *parented*!' I grin.

'In the extreme.' She nods. 'But the rewards are quite good. Tonight she's making lemon cake. I'll try to bring some to school tomorrow.' She hesitates on the corner, frowning. 'But can we really wait until tomorrow, Owl? Shouldn't we try to find him now?'

'Where, though?' I ask. 'We need to work out where to start, Mallory.'

'What about the Earl's world?'

That's exactly where we should be going. To the world where everything is autumn and the Earl is unchallenged king, just as Jack is in his winter realm. The incantation in the book of fae should work like a portal – there's magic in the words. Alberic used it last winter to get us to Jack's world, and without it I don't know how to get there. And honestly, I'm not even sure Alberic would be there.

'I'll take another look at the book this evening,' I say. 'But we might have to think of some other way to find him.' I turn and give her a hug. 'Thank you for today.'

'We're in this together,' she says. 'I mean it, Owl. I'm as worried as you are. I'll call you later.'

'I should've called you more, before,' I say. 'When you needed me. I really am sorry.'

'It's OK,' she says. 'I didn't make it easy, Owl. We should put it all behind us now.'

'OK,' I say, smiling. It's still hot and we haven't solved anything yet, but I breathe just a little bit easier than I have for weeks. At least we're a 'we' again.

5

'Owl!' Mum is fluttering by the front door when I get in, and she does not look happy. I dart around her into the flat and she follows me through to the kitchen. 'Where have you been?'

'I met up with Mallory,' I say.

'And how was that?' she asks. 'Could you not have let me know where you were going? What about your phone? Or an old-fashioned note, even?'

'I'm sorry.'

'I'm glad you're getting on again.' She smiles, but it quickly turns to a frown as she picks little bits of those cursed vines off my back. 'Owl? Have you been to the court?'

'The—'

'The old copse, where the fae court is. You know

where I mean.' She leans up against the counter and I notice the grey wires in her dark hair. 'After last winter, we had a deal. You were to tell me everything. No more late-night adventures.'

'There haven't been!'

'But you've been searching for him?'

She means Jack. They never met, last winter. She used to talk of him in a dreamy haze, and my power was magic that made her eyes spark. He knows he is my father and he knows who I am, what I'm capable of. But he never stayed around to find out about our lives. Never came to see her.

'No,' I say carefully. 'That's not what we were doing.'

Though that *is* part of what's powering my new determination. Yes, we need to find Alberic and get autumn going, whether that means finding the Earl or some other magical cure. But also I need to find Jack. I want winter, to have the thrill of the ice on my skin again. I want to feel the adventure of it all.

'But it *is* something fae related?' Mum demands, snapping me back.

'I said before that Alberic hasn't been at school. He isn't at home either – that's what we were doing today. He's missing,' I say after a long silence. 'And he doesn't have a human family out here to search for him, so we're it. Me and Mallory.'

Her eyes soften.

'You don't think he's just with his father?'

'I don't think so,' I say. 'And, even if he is, that doesn't help. Because autumn's missing – isn't it? – which means that the Earl is missing too.'

'And you're on a mission to find them.' She shakes her head with a pale, unwilling smile. 'Of course you are.' She reaches for the old stone teapot and the little cups, and I watch her as she makes jasmine tea. Her movements are slow and methodical and I know she's taking her time, trying to choose her next words.

'The thing is –' she sighs, motioning for me to sit opposite her – 'none of the usual rules work, do they? I've looked it up on all the forums, and it's useless, Owl. Everyone's all about *should this* and *should that* – they say you're just testing your boundaries with all this going out and about, that I need to let you learn things for yourself. They're all so sure, but I'm not!'

'What forums?' I stare at her. She never seemed to care much what other people thought before.

'The parenting ones.'

I bite my grin, but she sees it anyway.

'I wanted some advice!' she says.

'But there were no sections on children who are half fae?'

'No!' she howls, throwing her head back.

I pour the tea and push one of the cups towards her. The dragons on the sides are still, forever chasing their tails. Maybe that's how she feels. Maybe we need new cups.

We drink in silence for a while and I don't know how to start the conversation. Eventually, she does it instead.

'So. I am proud of you. I think you are amazing,' she says, making my eyes smart. 'I know you'll keep having these adventures. And my . . . issue with Jack is nothing to do with you. I'm sorry he disappoints you, that he isn't constant. I suppose that's his nature. It's frustrating, but it is also a beautiful, rare thing – as you are. But you are my girl, you are only thirteen, and you *have* to check in with me when you are having these adventures. I know you'll search for Alberic and I believe you'll find him. I worry about what else you'll find along the way. Are you ready?'

I stare at her.

'There's more than one way to be lost,' she says. 'I

saw it in Alberic last winter. Are you ready to find him, and find him different?'

'He'll be all right,' I say. 'We just need to get him home.'

'What is his home, though?' she asks. 'Does he want to be there?'

My heart thumps. How does she *always* hit on the thing that I've been hiding from?

'I thought we'd find him first and then we'd sort it out,' I say.

She blows her breath out slowly. 'OK. I'll be here.' She looks me in the eye. 'I mean it, Owl. No matter what happens, what you find . . . come back to me, and I'll be here.'

'Is that . . . Do you think I wouldn't come home again?'

'While you're chasing around in magical worlds of fae, where anything is possible, and everything is starlight-beautiful?' She laughs. 'It may have occurred to me. *I* got lost there for a while, after all, many years ago.'

'But this is home!' I raise the cup. 'See? Home!'

She leaps up from the table and hauls me out of the chair. I'm getting a bit old for these nose-crushing hugs of hers, but she smells of warm things and safety, and it fills me up, so I don't pull away.

I've smuggled *Fablef and Earth-Fpiritf* back to my room again while Mum paces, working in the attic overhead. I have a little ceremony before I try again to open it. I open the window, smooth the wooden feathers of the owl on my bedpost and go around the room touching all the owl sketches I've drawn over the years, as if somehow it will summon Mother Earth.

'*Mother Earth, ruler of all fae. Come to me. Show me the words where all the fae can be found*,' I whisper as I go. And then I open the book and it's *still* just blank pages. What is going on? For a moment the whole room seems to swoop and darken around me as if I've lost my footing and a door has been slammed in my face. What was so magical last winter feels like a trick now, my childish imagination believing a book could do magic. I thought there would always be a fae world to escape to, when this one got too hard. Always a place where fairies and sprites dance, where elementals playfight and tease. Maybe even a father in Jack Frost, even if he's not the sort of father anyone would have imagined.

And it's all gone. Even the book.

I slam it shut now and shove it under the blanket at the end of my bed. There *must* be another way through. I stare at the window and remember all the times last winter that Jack knocked against it and we rushed out together, turning the town to an icy wonderland. Icicles from every window, loops and whorls of ice up lamp posts and the fine fur of frost on the rooftops.

It was magical. It *was*. And I need it back. Somehow.

6

Mallory meets me in the lane the next day and she hasn't done that for ages, so it feels extra good to be falling back into step with her. Like the old days, even if everything else is different. Even if *we're* different.

'Hey,' she says. 'Welcome to another day of summer!' She's already got her sleeves rolled up, her hair twisted back away from her face. Her blazer hangs over her shoulder, hooked on her thumb.

'I'm over it,' I say as we trail along the main road. The cars make dust spin in their wake, and golden heat is already rising from the pavements. My breath feels tight and hard, and my bag keeps smacking into my back.

'I couldn't get that treehouse out of my head, Owl,' Mallory says after a while. 'I couldn't stop trying to imagine what it was like for him last year, coming to school and then going home to that . . . D'you think he was lonely? I mean, he lived on his own. Looked after himself. What must that be like?'

'I don't know,' I say.

'Well, something's gone horribly wrong. Did you manage to find anything out last night? We can't hold off much longer.'

'I know,' I say. 'But the book still isn't working, Mallory. I looked again last night and it was just the same – all blank.' I'm trying to sound calm, but it was my last hope. No Jack. No Alberic. No autumn. No court. No book. 'I don't know what else we can do . . .'

'Let's try again later,' she says. 'You would've been worn out yesterday, after all the court business. It's a new day. We'll do it together. That worked for us yesterday.'

'OK,' I say. Now Mallory's on the case, anything seems possible. Or at least it will be if I can stop feeling so tired all the time and actually do something worthwhile.

Like finding a friend who got lost without me even noticing.

*

The rest of the day passes in a dazed blur. I try to breathe slow and steady, filling my water bottle up between each lesson, and it's manageable. But it won't be for much longer. The winter in my veins is starving and I'm not sure I can live without it. Mallory sticks close in lessons, but we're not in all the same classes. It's during French that things start to get strange.

The languages classrooms are old Portakabins that hunch by the side of the main building. They're freezing in winter and boiling in summer – right now the one I'm in is like a furnace. I'm sitting by the window and when I first see her I think it must be an illusion. Or I'm asleep and it's a dream.

So I pinch myself.

But when I look back at the window she's still there, hair pink as candyfloss, cloak trailing over the dusty playground, coming closer. I can smell her, even through the glass – the scent of spring washing over me like cool water.

The Queen of May smiles and waves. Drifting away to the corner of the field, just visible, she sits on the outflung branch of an old sycamore tree. A small group of tiny brown bunnies gathers on the ground around her, picking through the pale blossoms that drift from her fingers. It's a fantasy postcard scene, with spring herself come to visit, but it's making my skin prickle. What is she doing here? Did she hear me talking to the owl last night? Did Mother Earth do something to bring her to me? I roll my eyes at myself and slide down in my seat. Last winter I fought her, and she is *not* a friend. She nearly ousted Jack entirely from the court, working with the Earl of October to disrupt the seasons.

And that's *exactly* what's happening again, right now. Does she have something to do with it?

When I look back, she's right at the window, long fingers spread out across the glass. She wears a smile of sweetest spring promise, but the snap of impatience in her eyes is chilling.

'Come out, little Owl,' she says.

I look around the room. Nobody else has noticed her and it's another ten minutes until the lesson ends. There's no way Queenie is waiting that long.

She taps against the window and a spiral of cool air filters through the classroom. Miss Pennington fans at her face with the French textbook.

'Owl?' she asks as I get out of my seat, picking up my bag. 'What are you doing?'

'I just need some air,' I say, my skin getting even hotter as the rest of the class turns to look. 'Please?'

She frowns at me.

'You do look a little peculiar. Very well. Report to student reception.'

'Yes, Miss Pennington.'

I charge out of the classroom and down the steps before anyone can stop me. Ice is creeping up the back of my neck and down my arms, but in this weather it instantly melts.

'I see this hot spell isn't doing you much good,' the Queen says, looking rather happy about it as I draw her away from the classrooms, hoping nobody's watching me. The back of the school field is lined with trees and I lead her there, into the shade. The bunnies hop after us and tiny pink-tinged daisies appear in the ground around her where she treads.

'It doesn't seem to be doing you any favours, either,' I retort, watching as the flowers turn instantly to brown dust. 'What are you doing here?'

'Considering,' she says with a sigh, looking up at the aching blue sky. 'This summer is getting boring.'

'You're not the only one to think that,' I say. 'Did you have something to do with it?'

She laughs, and the high, piping sound makes my ears wince.

'*Me?*' she asks, fanning at her face with one pale hand. 'My dear, you do give me credit!'

'Are you saying it's not you then, causing this?' I try to keep my voice level but it's hard to keep calm. She may look sweet but she's fierce, and I'm not sure I should be pressing her at all with my powers so weak.

'I'm not saying anything. You seem to be the one with all the sayings at the moment.'

'What do you want?' I ask.

'I want an end to it,' she says. 'It has gone on too long.'

'Perhaps if you could tell me how?' I ask. 'I've been trying to find a way to fix it but the book isn't working and I don't know how else to get to autumn . . .'

'The book –' she rolls her eyes, settling down on to the dry grass, pulling me with her. Her hand is cool, but it grips like a vice – 'is a human construct. No power in it. It isn't a portal. You should know that.'

'But . . . I've been able to get to places before, with the incantation.'

'An incantation.' She frowns. 'Now that is more interesting than a book. Did you activate it alone?'

I don't answer, realizing that actually I never managed to get anywhere with it, on my own. It was Alberic who read the words last time, and I was sitting right by him. Perhaps it was a combination of our power, then?

'They take more than a little power,' she says, and leans in close, patting my knee. Her scent is dizzying against the warp of heat in the air. 'However you do it, do it you must, and soon. I need you to find your friend.'

'Alberic?'

'That's the one,' she says. Across the field, the bell rings for lunch, and kids start spilling from the wide school doors. 'Poor Alberic.'

I frown. Sympathy doesn't look natural on her face. Does she know where he's gone?

'Why poor?'

'Have you never thought so?' she asks. She runs her fingers over the scorched ground and it swells with new green grass. 'He is fragile, is he not?' The grass withers when she removes her hand and she sighs. 'You have much of the ice of your father in you, Owl, if you have not realized it already.'

The comparison stings. One of the hardest things about having Jack Frost for a father is how inhuman he is. All the things I hoped for in a father, all the little dreams I had, well, they're just not going to happen. I tell myself it doesn't matter because he's *Jack Frost* and I've inherited his powers, which is awesome. But sometimes, actually, it would just be nice to have a second parent to talk to, and to buy you cake after school. Or unicorns called Eugene. Or even to acknowledge that you're their daughter – he never really has. He thinks he can't be a father to a human girl. Is that the kind of friend I am? Careless, and fickle?

'I've been trying to find him,' I say weakly.

'Have you?' she asks. 'Well, it's about time. Why have you not succeeded?'

'It's hard to get in the court – Lady Midday has taken it over.'

'So she has.' The Queen sighs. 'But you do have some power, little Owl. And if you need more there are still friends in the court, though they may be rather quiet.' She frowns at the bunnies, who sit in the shade now, their eyes dull. 'It is no good this horrible summer, for friend or foe.'

'*Did* you have something to do with it?' I ask again.

'No, my dear. Well, perhaps I planted the seed. I could not have foreseen what would happen next. That old fool went further than I could have imagined –

and the young one disappeared after! I don't know where . . .' She glares at me. 'And I shall not be searching for them; I have other things to do. Our sweet Lady Midday has got her claws into this world and she will not let go until she has to. It is all I can do now to weather this storm. There is no way out, for any of us fae.'

'What does all that mean?' I demand. 'No way out?'

'We have been cut off,' she says. 'This old book you've been talking about is probably blank because there is no way in or out of our worlds. Those who are in them are trapped within, and those without . . . are trapped here.' She looks around with a sour expression. 'You must try again to find the spell that opens worlds. I was fighting Lady Midday and her summer off for too long. I stayed when I should have gone to my world, and now I'm stuck as you are. Except that you, being only *half* fae, can do something about it.'

'What do you mean?'

'It's a stalemate,' she says. 'None of the fae can get in or out – someone has broken the rules.'

'Were you the one who broke the rules?'

She laughs. 'It does sound like me, doesn't it? But no, my dear. This one is not on me.'

'So what *did* happen?' I demand. 'Where is Alberic? What did you do to him?'

'I've already told you – are you not listening? I gave him one of my seeds,' she says. 'The Earl is slow to forgive – he did not appreciate Alberic meddling in his affairs last year. We had our cunning plan, to be rid of Jokul, and between the two of you it was ruined.' She sighs. 'Order maintained, all as it should be. *Boring*. You half-fae are fragile things, and Alberic could not live with the Earl's disapproval. He sought change in his father's heart, so I gave him one of spring's finest seeds, because I thought it would be entertaining to see what happened. He went off to plant it on the Earl and it has changed . . . *everything*.' She shrugs and doesn't try to hide her proud little smile. 'They are powerful, my seeds.'

'Maybe you should be more careful with them, then,' I say hotly.

She laughs at me. 'You do have some of the wiles of your father about you. Is that why you left your boy to his own torment? Did you even see it? Jack was never much good at friendship, either. Ah! Speaking of friends, here is your sweet little human. Is she your conscience, little Owl?'

I turn from her and see Mallory heading in our direction.

'Hey,' she says, dropping down to sit with us. 'What's going on?'

I wonder if the Queen can see the fear in her eyes. The minute gestures that show me Mallory is not nearly as comfortable as she's making out. It's not surprising – ever since last winter she's been the only human able to see the court, or any of the fae.

'I heard you might need some help finding your dear friend Alberic,' the Queen says.

'Is that what you're offering?' Mallory asks bluntly.

'Yes, is it?' I demand. 'Do you have *any* idea where he is? You said the spell opens worlds – what world is he *in*?'

The Queen blinks, and her eyes turn dark as storm clouds.

'Silly children,' she hisses. 'You think to speak to me thus, as if I could not turn your simple lives upside down in a flash. I sought you out on a whim – I had forgotten how often I regret those. Your friend was misled by such a moment. He is with *Time*.' She rises, her cloak spilling bright blossoms that turn brown and wilt as soon as they touch the ground, turns and sweeps away.

'What does that mean?' groans Mallory, flopping on to the grass. 'Is there some sort of time person? Clockman, or something. Sundial . . .'

'Mr Sundial!' I call out, scrambling up. The whole idea is ridiculous, but then so is everything else. We're just making wild stabs in the dark. 'Show yourself!'

Mallory stares at me, outraged.

'Clockman!' I howl, turning in the field, searching the branches of the wilting trees. 'Where are you?'

'Stop it.' Mallory jostles me, grinning as my voice rises into hysterical laughter. 'I don't see why it's that silly – you have the Green Man, and Lady Midday . . .'

'Far too much of her,' I say. 'Does this endless summer really not feel that bad to you, Mall?'

'I mean, it's too warm,' she concedes as we head back into school. 'And I miss wearing cardigans and boots and things.'

'But it doesn't feel like everything's dying?'

'Is that how it feels to you?'

'A bit. When was the last time there was rain out here?' I ask. 'Can you remember? It's not good, Mallory.'

'Course it's not,' she says. 'But we already knew that. For years summer has been getting hotter and longer – now she's really excelled herself, apparently with the

Queen of May's help. We were already on our way to find Alberic and see if we could fix it all – at least now we know the Queen had something to do with it.'

'She gave Alberic one of her seeds of change, she said. And now everyone's locked in and out of worlds . . . except maybe me.'

'Maybe you?'

'She said something about how I was the one who might be able to get through, since I'm half fae. And there's this world-opening spell, which must be the incantation in the book. We'll have to try it,' I say. 'Now we know what we're looking for.'

'A magical sundial!' Mallory says, stifling laughter.

The book of *Fablef and Earth-Fpiritf* seems to get heavier every time I handle it. Mum's busy in the studio over our heads and, whatever it is she's doing, it doesn't seem to be going terribly well – she's doing a lot of thump-striding and it feels a bit like being in a drum.

'Is she wearing clogs?' Mallory asks as we settle down on the settee with the book. 'What is she doing?'

'Pacing.' I laugh. 'They're old cowboy boots; they're supposed to be inspirational.'

'Maybe for Christmas you should get her some

inspirational slippers.'

'With unicorns on.'

'Exactly!' She grins as I put the book on the table in front of us and flap open the front cover. For an old, heavy book, it's surprisingly sturdy. I take a deep breath as Mallory picks it up and starts flicking the pages.

'Magic,' Mallory says with a sparkle in her eyes. 'Isn't it beautiful!'

Mallory's a big book lover. She's been known to choose them just for the cover, or for funny crinkled page edges, or because they have a ribbon in them. She reaches forward now and turns the pages reverently.

'What can you see?' I ask from behind my hands. 'It's not blank?'

'No – why aren't you looking?'

'It must have only been blank for me! If I look, maybe it'll go away again.' I close my eyes and try to see the book the way it used to be, but it's hopeless. She's going to have to work it out.

'So . . . why would it be working for me?' she asks. 'Maybe because I'm human, so it's just an old book? Oh, but look at the font on the lettering! And that colour in the illustration, Owl! I didn't know it had pictures.'

'It doesn't!' I say, still behind my hands. 'Look for a

time figure, Mallory. Time. Sundials and clocks, and . . .'

'Fathers!' she crows. 'Father Time, that's who we're looking for! I *knew* there was a time figure! I just couldn't remember – that Queen is very confusing.'

'Yes, she is,' I say. 'And somehow she's involved in all of this, which means anything could have happened to Alberic. So we know what world we're heading for – can you see an incantation?'

'Wait a minute. Let's read this . . . There's a beautiful picture of a little boy; he's playing with toy cities. They look like what I saw in the lake, Owl! And he doesn't look so scary. What does it say . . .' Her voice drops, and she begins to read.

FATHER TIME

In one word: chaos. How can there be order in a world where Time is fluid? Where a moment can last a lifetime, where the future is as real as the past and there is no present?

Father Time is not welcome in the world of Mother Earth. He plays with the natural order of all living things, and all living things are at his mercy.

In the world of Time, cities are born to fall in moments. moments themselves are shadowy things, hooded and cloaked; they are not real, for nothing is real there. They are illusions, Father Time's own creations. And as he has created them, they have no substance.

Time has no substance; it is fleeting and fickle, and its father is the very cruellest of fae, for life and death mean nothing, when the past is not the past.

7

'We have to get there,' Mallory says, snapping the book shut and pulling me to my room, where we perch on the bed. 'Let's try, Owl.'

'Now?'

'If he's there, we can't wait. This place sounds hideous and we don't know how long Alberic's already been there.'

Last winter, Alberic got us to Jack's icy world by reading the incantation. We arrived in a flurry of snow and ice and were chased by the wolves of winter, before he nearly died of the cold and Jack rescued us. I managed to get us home using my magic and the very last of my energy, but that was when it was winter and my power was full. It was hard enough for us to finally make it to the court yesterday – I'm not sure I have enough left in me to take us to a new world, ruled by a figure I'd never even heard of before now, especially if I can't see the words myself.

'Let's try this incantation, then,' I say. 'It should be at the front of the book.'

Mallory shuffles back through the pages and my blood starts to race in my veins. If the Queen is right, this may all go horribly wrong. But everything she and Mum said about Alberic rings too true. I *know* he needs help and I would do anything to get to him.

'OK,' Mallory says. 'I've got it. Ready?'

I nod as she reaches for me. Her skin is cool and dry against mine and her voice steady as she begins to read. I squeeze my eyes closed and try to conjure that feeling of power, of ice. Mallory gasps, and my skin starts to burn – it's not right. It's not supposed to feel like that . . .

'Owl!'

'Too hot!' I mutter. Something damp slaps at my forehead and I push it away, opening my eyes.

'I was so worried!' Mallory sits back. 'Keep the flannel on – you're burning up.'

My head aches. I pull myself up against the

headboard and stare from her to the book.

'It didn't work,' I say.

'It did not.' She sighs.

'How long's it been?'

'You've been raving for about half an hour,' she says. 'What a nightmare. I am never trying that again.'

'It's OK. I'm fine,' I say, sitting up.

'I'm not sure you really are,' she says. 'The trouble is you won't be until we find autumn, and to find autumn we need to get answers, and to get *answers* we need to get to Time . . .'

'We could try the court again,' I say, remembering the Lady's words and feeling the sting of them once more. She *said* the fae part of me meant nothing and now it has failed me entirely. I'm not going to give up so easily, though. 'My power isn't enough to make the incantation work, especially right now. Lady Midday isn't there all the time, and the Queen said there were still friends in the court. If we snuck back in with the book, we might be able to get help from the Green Man – at least we know where he is . . .'

'It's worth a try,' she says doubtfully. 'We can't be doing that again, that's for sure.'

'What a nightmare, all over a stupid seed,' I say.

'A seed of change,' intones Mallory. 'Do you think he'd have used it, Owl, if we'd been around for him more? If he was less lonely, he might not have even tried to change the Earl. Anyone who's met him would know he can't be changed!'

'But it's his dad,' I say, my mind going uneasily to Jack, knowing how much it hurts to be faced with some elemental fae figure who seems too large for real life. Too large to be a parent. 'I get it.'

She grunts. 'How do you feel now?'

'Hot and thirsty,' I say. 'Which isn't a lot different, to be honest. What about you?'

'Oh, just like I almost killed my best friend, that's all.'

Her eyes are glittering, and I realize I've never really seen Mallory frightened before. I reach forward and pull her into a hug.

'Really,' I say. 'It's OK. I'm sorry I worried you.' She lies down by my side and we stare up at the ceiling.

'Remember the time you froze my bedroom?'

I grin, and turn the flannel so the cool side is against my brow. 'Your mum was not impressed.'

'It all melted and she thought we'd had a water fight in there!'

*

We lie there for ages, while the day turns to night, reminiscing, and then I wake and she's gone. The window is wide open and the darkness outside is calling to me. I check the time. It's 2 a.m. The coolest part of the day. I lie there for a while staring at the window, remembering nights when I'd nip out to join Jack and we'd dance through the streets. *Little Owl*, he'd call me and I hated it. But there was a grin on his face when he said it, and I never heard him speak to anyone else quite like that.

Where are you? I sigh, staring at the place where he'd been the last time he called for me. The stars glimmer in the heat. On a sudden urge I slide off the bed and hook my legs over the windowsill, dropping to the ground.

Then I run.

8

The last time I came out with Jack was at the end of February, when the snowdrops and the crocuses made him snarl. Spring was coming and there was a sadness in him that made him wilder than ever. He leaped higher, ran faster, danced like there was no tomorrow.

I suppose there wasn't, not for him.

That night, though, I wasn't worried about what was coming and how long he'd be gone. I wasn't worried about anything. We'd saved the world back before Christmas and I was revelling in my new powers, already sensing they'd not last much longer.

'You must rest a little through the spring and summer,' Jack had said. 'So that you may come back into your power when the Earl of October has done his business.'

'What about you?'

'I'll be in my world of winter, little Owl.'

'Can I visit?'

He hesitated, and that was enough. *No*, that hesitation said. *You don't belong there.* But I didn't truly *belong* in either world. I wasn't wholly human, or fae. I was something in between. Just as Alberic felt out of place in the human world, I felt out of place with my magic, here, with my own father. We were coming from opposite sides of the same problem.

So I was angry as we headed through town, keeping to the shadows, past the school and the clocktower and over an ancient stone bridge, Jack pretty much dancing the whole way. I'm not sure it's possible for him to walk like a normal person.

'Where are we going?' I demanded as the old castle loomed into view. 'This place? You can't be serious, Jack. Why are we here?'

'Old stone,' he said. 'Nothing better to keep the sun out than good old stone. Come on, nobody lives here!'

He looked so gleeful. He was bouncing on his feet, mirror eyes flashing.

'Isn't it locked up? It's a tourist attraction, Jack – you can't just break in!'

'But,' he said, 'I can!'

He vaulted over the stile to the car park and headed for a small door to the side of the locked iron gates, producing a key from his pocket.

'You have a *key*?' I asked, clambering with a lot less grace over the stile.

'It is the easiest way,' he said, turning it in the lock and motioning me inside. 'Don't you think?'

'I thought you'd freeze the lock!'

'No, little Owl. Waste of my energy.'

'What about CCTV?'

'See see you pardon me?'

I sighed. 'Security cameras!'

'Ah, electricity. That doesn't work around me, my dear. Do not worry.'

'I don't think this is a very good idea . . .'

But he's wasn't listening – he never does. He danced forward, through a courtyard with a grand old fountain and into a wide corridor, where iron sconces lined the walls. The dark eyes of old nobility stared out at us from oil portraits behind little red ropes, and there were glass-covered signs on the walls, with maps and information written beneath. Jack skipped past it all, leaving icy footprints behind him, and I registered the familiar prickle of frost sweeping up the back of my neck. The air was cool; the stone walls, when I reached out, were like a blast of energy, cold and smooth against my palms.

'Better, little Owl?'

'A little bit,' I said.

'You're a creature of the world,' he said, nodding. 'The way you're feeling is spring coming . . . the end of our season. Better not to ignore such things.'

'Because I'm your daughter?'

He turned and stared at me. I'd rarely put it so bluntly before and my stomach dropped as I looked into his eyes. I shouldn't challenge him like that.

But I did.

'Because you are half-fae,' he said.

'Jack?'

'Owl?'

'Please? Why don't you like it? Do you really still have *any* doubt, after everything that's happened?'

He turned and marched into the main room of the castle. There was a roped-off heavy wooden table at its centre. A meal had been set out, with plastic pig heads and whole fake chickens. The scene froze as I stood in the doorway; the floor became an ice rink, the walls glittering with frost. The iron chandeliers swayed with the weight of Jack's work.

'Because you are you.' He skated up to me, looking as inhuman as a creature can look, his skin glinting with traces of frost, his hair thick with ice. 'Now come. Play.'

I ventured on to the ice, breathing in the frozen air deeply. Something unlocked inside my chest as I did and I began skating. Dodging the darts that came from Jack, I sent a few of my own, more and more until it was a fight across the table, fast and furious. I didn't give in – I just kept fighting, harder and harder. He grinned and told me it was a powerful mix, the fae and the human: fae for power, humanity for perseverance. I hardly listened, I was so furious with him. By the end of the evening I was still angry and he was just sad. He saw me back to the flat and walked away with lowered shoulders, ice curling in the air as he went.

And that was the last time I saw him.

Months later I follow the same path towards the castle, wondering whether this time I'll have the courage to fight my way inside. Wondering if the old stone will feel cool, even in the still-warm murk of night. I can almost see the shadow of my former self here with him and wish that night had gone differently. I wish I'd asked him more about the summer and when to expect him. I wish I'd told him that I needed him. When I get to the gates, they are wide open. Lady Midday is there, standing in a heat haze and a golden burst of light, her cloak spread across the courtyard, her goblin and sprite minions perched on the castle's window ledges like gargoyles.

'Owl,' she says. 'I thought I was clear when we spoke yesterday. When I told you to let your humanity see you through this, I meant you should stay at home, out of my way.'

I put one hand out to the cold castle wall beside me and gather my magic, the images of that last night with Jack still clear, lending me power, and send a bolt of ice towards her. It drifts wide of its mark, and melts even while it's still in the air.

'Human like that?' I ask, knowing I'm being reckless and still wanting more. I'm tired of this heat, of the games of the fae. Tired of waiting and always feeling weaker, smaller.

'If you like,' she says, clapping her hands. 'Are you ready, little Owl?'

'Don't call me that.' I bite the words out, one hand

still on the wall, glad for the ache of cool against my palm. I don't know what to expect from this spectre, on the street beneath the moon. I've danced with Jack and with Boreas, the North Wind. I've faced down the Earl of October with Alberic, but I've never gone head to head like this, and if I fight with what scant ice and frost I can dredge up from the very core of myself, what will she fight with?

It turns out that she'll fight with fire.

A whip of pure sunlight and a blast of heat that throws me off my feet before we've even begun. I untangle myself from the white-hot streak and push at her with all I have. For an instant, she is held in a blizzard. Her skin dims, her hair is coated in frost. But she is Lady Midday, she is a whole *season* and I am just me, so with a casual flick of her shoulders she is through it, cinder-bright, and I am light-headed from exertion.

She doesn't hold back. Heat comes at me like a thick, choking cloud and the whip unfurls and snaps at my feet, its tip flicking up to my shoulders. I bite down a yelp of pain and surprise and fight back, digging deep to bring a downpour of hail that falls in sharp pings to the street. The Lady shields her face with one outflung arm, slipping and staggering as she moves forward. She raises her head and her eyes are full-black. The air before her smoulders, evaporating the ice in an instant. I push forward once more, straining against the heat that sucks my energy and makes me want to howl.

So I howl. I think of Alberic and Mallory, my mother and the whole town suffering at the whim of this creature who will *never* give up, not until she absolutely has to. I push with everything inside me, stretching my arms wide, my fingers flexed.

The ground beneath our feet becomes ice. The street fills with the pale mist of it, fractals spinning, and she shudders as fine threads of frost weave up her legs.

'You are impossible!' she growls, throwing it off as she stalks towards me. She comes closer until I can smell the warp of the air around her, like the stench of melting tarmac. I move back until I'm trapped between the castle wall and her fury. 'You are dangerous,' she hisses. 'I sought you here to see for myself, and it is clear. The power of seasons in humanity – it is wrong. You will use all your body, all your heart, you fight with everything, against all order, where fae would know when they are *beaten*!' A surge of heat folds over me. 'No wonder the Earl despairs at his son, if he is like you. Half fae, half human – you are not fit for either world. Be warned, little Owl: the next time we meet, I will not be playing.'

And with that she turns, gathering her hordes with a flick of her spiralling fire-hair, and the street glows as she goes, every window molten flame, every tree burnished. It lingers, long after she's gone, and so does the heat.

'Well, nor will I!' I shout through the darkness, far too late for her to actually hear. 'I'll get back into that court,' I mutter to myself. 'I'll get in there and I'll find a way to Time and I'll get Alberic, and then we'll both fight to end your horrible reign. And if the Earl and Jack don't show up to help then that will be fine because we'll be fine because we will FIGHT ANYWAY, because it isn't supposed to be SUMMER any more and you're cheating!'

I storm from the castle and once again see myself as I was at the end of winter, when I was with Jack. He didn't count on all of this – none of us did. And now it's on me and Mallory to sort it out, and we will. I can't worry about the whys or the hows.

We just have to do it.

FICKLE FAE

Much has been written of the fair folk, and nearly all of it is true, no matter how contradictory, because the fae do not abide by rules as humans do. Their lives are not counted in years; their deeds defy logic. They have walked the earth for thousands of years, and they rule the corners of the world where man has rarely gone.

Under water they are kings and queens; on mountain passes they hold court. They are present and hidden in every inch of woodland; in sand dunes they play, in gardens they dance – each tiny scrap of grass has seen fairy feet. There is no flower that has not been touched, no leaf unturned. The

fae despair of mankind's carelessness, and yet, to mankind,
they are fickle, inconstant, often even cruel. They are wild
and they do not care for our standards. They care for theirs,
and theirs are far beyond our understanding.

9

It's evening, and Mallory and I have both made our excuses at home. She told her dad we're having a late picnic, to make the most of the last of this infernal weather. And I told Mum that we were going to spend the evening plotting for a way to find Alberic, so that was half true. I packed soda bread, cheese and some lentil crisps. It was all going fairly well until Mum found me leaving with the book and quite sharply took it off me.

'What are you doing with this?' she demanded. 'I thought you were meeting Mallory for a picnic?'

'She likes the book,' I'd blurted. 'We thought we'd look at it . . .'

'You and I both know that this isn't just a sweet book about fairy tales,' Mum said. 'It's not to leave the house, Owl.'

'We weren't about to get jam on it!'

'What *were* you about to do, then?' she asks, hefting the book into her arms.

There was no good answer to that, so I headed off without the book for my picnic, fuming.

It's quite a nice picnic, considering. Mallory's brought apples and little iced cakes, and she didn't seem that surprised when I told her what had happened about the book. In fact, she almost looked a bit relieved.

'We'll try anyway,' I say through a mouthful of lentil-crisp sandwich.

Mallory tips her head back and stares up at the blue sky.

'Without the book?' she asks.

'It might work,' I say. 'I did have a word with the owl.'

'The owl?'

'The wooden one on the bedpost. Sometimes Mother Earth is listening there.'

'So we're hoping she was listening today?'

'Yep. Hoping she was listening, and that she'll keep Lady Midday distracted somehow, so that we can get into the court and find the extra power we need to get to Time. I had planned on bringing the book with the incantation, obviously, but the Green Man might know the words. We can ask him to help us with the power too, and then we can bring Alberic home.'

'Do you think he can do autumn alone, without the Earl?'

'I'm not sure. I don't know that I could make winter happen without Jack. But I could do *something*. And we might find the Earl when we find Alberic, anyway.'

'Surely if he could come back on his own, he would.'

'But we don't know what happened to him when Alberic used that seed of change. Once we've got Alberic, we can work it out.'

'Once we've got Alberic,' Mallory says, moodily chomping into an apple. The sky is edging towards gold now, the heat just a caress rather than a full-on whack. 'You're sure about this, Owl? Nothing happened last time we were in there.'

I breathe out slowly. 'Let's just try.'

The way into the copse of trees is just as painful and difficult as it was last time, but today I don't care. I barely feel the sting of the vines, the gentle yet poisonous touch of the massive orange blooms. I remember my row with Lady Midday and let the anger stoke my power as I stride through, Mallory behind me. The Queen of May said there would be friends in here; it must be possible to reach them. Both of us are on guard for more dangerous things than foliage, and as the way gets darker, the claws of the vines get sharper. I push them away with the scant frost at my fingertips and finally, just as little black dots appear at the edge of my vision, we emerge next to the lake.

It's a green, swampy-looking puddle, buzzing with flies and filling the air with the sour smell of things long gone off. The stillness is even worse than last time; it's in the air, which is hard to breathe. I look around at Mallory, hauling her out of the last trapping branches, and we perch at the base of the Green Man for a moment, catching our breath, looking around. He isn't offering much help right now, and I can't see any other fae around.

'There must be a way. I wish we had the book!' I mutter, almost to myself.

'I remember it,' Mallory says quietly.

'Remember what?'

'The incantation.'

'Really? Why didn't you say?'

'It got burned into my brain the other day.' She

shakes her head. 'It's been running through my mind ever since. But I'm not sure we should use it, Owl.'

'It's worth a try,' I say. 'Last time we were here, I felt him shift.' I jab my elbow into the thick bark of the Green Man. 'He's not completely asleep. I *know* he isn't. I think he'll help us, if he knows what we're doing. If he knows we're trying to rescue *Alberic* from *Time*.' I emphasize the words, hoping that he can hear. That somehow I can harness his power to get us where we need to be.

'Why have they all just abandoned this place anyway?' she asks. 'I mean, why don't they wake and fight her? Why aren't *they* looking for Alberic, or the Earl?'

'Maybe they did for a while,' I say. 'It's nearly November – who knows what's happened here over the last few months. Shall we try?' She looks worried, and I realize I'm asking a lot, especially when we're still in the early days of being friends again. 'We don't have to. *You* don't have to, Mallory . . .'

'I do,' she says decisively. 'I've got the words in my head. And if you're caught up in this, and Alberic is too, then so am I. We did it all together last year and it worked out. But you have to tell me to stop if it doesn't feel right.'

'Absolutely.'

I rest one hand against the gnarled grey wood of the Green Man, patting him and sending a little wish for him to hear, and Mallory takes my other hand, putting her free hand on to his trunk and reciting the words. A swell of something rushes through me as she speaks, and it's not my power, which is jagged and sluggish, but a rush of pure magic, like a heartbeat inside my own. I latch on to the rise and fall of Mallory's recitation and then the magic of the Green Man thunders, drowning everything out as the court disappears.

10

Mallory's fingers are tight round mine and everything around us is darkness. Cool air fills my lungs and I take the deepest breath I have for months, feeling it settle like a balm. Time is dark and cool, and for a moment it's a relief. But with the second breath my stomach lurches as the ground shifts beneath our feet, splintering and falling away. We stagger backwards as a yawning hole opens up where we landed, and then there's a BOOM that reverberates through my skull.

We are on dark marshland, and the air is grey mist across a broad, flat horizon. There's nothing but us, as far as we can see, until with another lurch a mountain is born, in an upward cascade of rock and earth. It settles and immediately begins to fall to dust. In its wake, a city grows. One dark stone house, lightless, featureless.

Then another, and another, taller, broader, unfolding like dominoes, only to fall again.

'What is happening?' Mallory asks. 'Is this what all the worlds are like, Owl?'

'No,' I breathe. 'Jack's is winter – there are wolves . . .'

'So time is . . .'

'Time is a series of moments,' comes a whisper behind us. We turn to see a wraith-like shadow approaching, flickering in and out of existence, its voice like static. 'None of it is real. It's just games he plays; centuries happening in moments. Nothing really lives here.'

'Who are you?'

'One such moment.' The wraith comes closer, its cloak flapping, pale face shining beneath the hood. Its dark eyes widen as it takes us in, and then it flickers, and vanishes.

'All that is here is a moment,' says another, stepping towards us through the mist that shifts and clings to its form. This one is smaller, eyes bright. 'We are all just one of his thoughts, made into a moment of change. Time is a god here, and everything is possible. New worlds are born and obliterated just as fast. Nothing is permanent. See . . .' The figure gestures towards the glint on the horizon: a rolling grey sea that spits white foam out on to a pearly beach. Between one crashing wave and the next, the sea has receded, and when we look back to the figure it's gone.

The earth breaks again, a great chasm opening just before our feet. I grab Mallory and pull her back as grey stones clatter up in flashing layers to form a tower. A flicker of lightning, another BOOM and the tower blackens, becomes a ruin, crumbling to dust.

'Why are you here?' asks a small boy, crawling out of the wreckage. He is grey-skinned, his eyes flashing like mirrors, and his white hair is a starburst around his shoulders.

'Are you a moment?' Mallory asks in a thin voice.

The boy laughs and the world shudders with the sound. 'We are all moments,' he says, and now he is our age, and strikingly, terribly like Alberic. 'Don't you see? All the world is a moment.'

'But *you* aren't,' I say, because I've guessed who this is and I *know* I'm not wrong. Father Time is playing like Jack, quick and cruel. 'Stop playing. We're looking for our friend.'

'So . . . you are fae,' says the Alberic figure, only now much bigger, its face shadowed by a cloak. 'You must be Jokul's daughter. Well, well. All these half-human, half-fae children come to visit Time. Am I honoured? There never were such as you before, you know. You are *new*!' The word reverberates around us.

'I don't know about that,' I say. 'I only want to take Alberic home; we know he's here.'

'Does he have a home?' the figure asks, its eyes dark now, and sorrowful. 'He does not think he has one. What is a home, little Owl? What is a home, with neither mother nor father, nor friend either?'

'He has friends! He has a whole court of—'

'Ah! A court of fickle fae, who slumber through seasons not their own, and must work all the harder to keep the magic in a failing human world. Does that sound like home?'

'Home is love,' Mallory says, frowning. 'It can change, but if there is love . . .'

'Love . . .' The figure shrugs. 'Love is presence. Present, past and future. Love is a moment. Where were you when he needed you? When summer roared and his father turned his back and all the fae began to fade in the sun's harsh glare?'

'The Green Man and the Lady of the Lake . . . and Mother Earth. They love him.'

'But he is a *human* boy. More, or less. The love of fae

is fairweather. It is not home.'

Mallory's hand tightens round mine and I know her heart is thundering too, because it's exactly what we feared. He was alone. We had our summer holidays. She divided hers between her mum and her dad, and that was hard enough. I spent mine on a canal boat with Mum and laughed when every morning she had to clear the frost I'd made overnight off the tiller – it was cooler then, when summer was just in its infancy. Where did Alberic spend his? On the last day of school, when we said goodbye, he just smiled and said he'd see us in September. Why didn't we ask him what he'd be doing? Why didn't I visit?

'Where is he?' I demand.

'He is Lost.'

Father Time has shifted once more, grown to a towering giant of a man, and he looms over us now, a scythe in one hand and a storm shifting in his cloak, as around us the world turns to darkest night.

'Help us find him!' I order, determined not to show I'm afraid of him, no matter what he looks like.

He stoops to me.

'You never should have lost him, silly girl. You were so busy mourning all that you didn't have. Did you ever imagine that someone like Jack could truly be a father? How does your hope still burn so bright?'

I stare back at him, feeling magic stir in my veins. It's scary here, but the cool air feels good and my Jack Frost power, strong enough to freeze lakes last winter, is beginning to surge, lending me new courage. 'Where. Is. Alberic?'

Time laughs and then he's gone, and the land falls in front of us until we're on a toppling cliff, our feet skating on loose rocks. There's nothing to hold on to but each other, and so we cling as we fall. And, just as quickly, we're on cold, hard tiles – a promenade with palm trees that bow in a smoke-billowing wind.

'What's *this*?' Mallory whispers. 'Owl, this is a nightmare!'

'We just need to find him,' I say.

'But how? Nothing is real!'

'Just . . . keep moving. We know he's here – Father Time said he was.'

And now I'm feeling stronger. I'm furious with all these god-like figures who play such cruel games with us all. Time, Jack, the Earl, they're all more trouble than they're worth, but Alberic is here somewhere, and we're going to get him home.

11

We make our way along the promenade, which shifts to become a woodland trail, and then opens out to a desert. It's unrelenting and exhausting, every step taking us further into chaos. The strange, hooded moments appear and disappear, all beneath a grey sky where the clouds hustle. Here, where anything seems possible, it is possible that we could just wander forever, that my magic is just an illusion – a hope that could be dashed when I try to use it. I wonder if Alberic has felt this same pattern of hope and dread: of power, then of empty-headed fatigue. Just to stay on your feet here, you have to be on your guard every second.

Mallory grabs at me as another trench opens up before us, filling quickly with a seething white-foamed river. It snakes out across the ground and silver stars prick the sky.

'Cursed place,' I groan. 'Everything's changing all the time, Mallory!'

The river spreads, becomes a lake, and in the distance a lighthouse swirls up, a white tower that reaches high to the fading moon as the sky begins to brighten.

'It's horrible,' she says, shivering. 'And Alberic's been here for so long, Owl.'

It feels like hours. We fight our way through forests, shuffle through dusty sands, hop through the scrubby grass of dunes. For a while, it is light, the sun a golden ball in the sky, but then darkness falls again, and holes open up in an endless stretch of brittle grey land.

'What will we do if we can't find him?' Mallory asks eventually. 'Do you know how to get home?'

'Not without him.'

'You mean we can't get home without him?' She sounds horrified.

'I mean, we won't go without him,' I say, hoping it sounds more reassuring than I feel.

'Obviously,' she says. 'Only it would be good to know we can get out of here!'

'We can,' I say. I focus on the ground in front of us

and it freezes before our eyes. Just a thin layer of frost, but it sparks hope in me – my magic *is* here.

'You frosted!' Mallory says with a grin.

'Now if only we could find him . . . Alberic!' I shout, frost blooming out with my breath. For a moment, nothing. Just more of the same shifting horizon.

And then something familiar. A lamp post, on a path across a field. The same field that bounds the court! The light is golden, the lamp post tall and straight. A semblance of our world – and I didn't make it happen. This is somebody else's work, and it's very familiar.

'Here,' I say, pulling at Mallory. 'This is outside the court, where Alberic and I first walked. We talked about Jack Frost, before I knew anything . . . I'm sure it is.' The field disappears, the light in the lamp flickers and then swells. The lamp post itself stays. And there is a figure sitting beneath it, his back against the metal.

'Alberic?'

The lamp post disappears. A howling wind blows through us all, and ice sweeps over my skin as the figure struggles to stand. It *is* Alberic. Taller by a head now than any human boy and too thin, his chestnut hair falling to his waist in vine-like ropes.

'Moments,' he whispers. He closes his eyes, and

the lamp post begins to form. He's using *his* magic, I realize, to make something solid here, something familiar. I wonder how long he's been stuck here doing this. He looks utterly exhausted.

'No,' Mallory says. 'Do I look like a moment to you, Alberic?'

'Have you seen him?'

'Who?'

'My father. I've been looking.'

His eyes flash and Mallory rushes towards him as his knees give way, catching him as his head falls forward. He's too light; there's hardly any substance to him at all. What does happen to half-fae here? Maybe there's magic, but when was the last time he ate or drank?

'How do we get home, Owl?' Mallory whispers, frightened. I stare at her uneasily. If he couldn't do it, how will I? But . . . maybe he never tried, because he was still looking for the Earl. And we haven't been here for months like he has.

'Magic, I hope.'

'Do we need the incantation again?'

'Should've brought my red clicky shoes,' I murmur, thinking of home. I haven't travelled through fae worlds on my own before, and I'm not exactly sure about how to get back. Jack helped us get out of the world of winter last year, but he's not here now.

I can feel his power, though, getting stronger in my veins the longer we stand here in the cold wind.

'Can't leave,' Alberic mutters, pushing himself up and away from us, swaying on his feet. He looks alarmingly like the Earl in this strange twilight world, so tall and thin. He's stretched out and his skin is birch-silver. 'Not without him. I've been searching, but the moments are confusing me – I never seem to get anywhere . . .'

'Forget him,' I say. 'We need to get out of here now, Alberic. If we stay, we might never get home.'

'But we need him,' he says through gritted teeth. 'Isn't that why you're here? Because autumn is missing? It was my fault. It's all my fault . . .'

'We're here because *you* are missing,' says Mallory. 'And we need to get you home – this place is no good for you.'

He searches our faces. 'Not without him. I tricked him with the Queen's seed . . . It was a mistake, and I didn't know how to fix it. I came to find him, but I lost my way. Now you're here, we need to search. He's gone off, and I couldn't follow.' He shakes his head as a thicket of narrow, tin-tiled towers flashes up to one side of us. 'I think he's gone back in time.'

'What do you mean?'

'The seed of change,' he says. 'I planted it on him and he came here, so I followed. But I was too late – he'd already gone on and I wasn't strong enough to go after him.'

'Where did he go?'

'There's a place in this world, where you can get to the past . . .' He gestures through the murk, but it's impossible to see through it. Impossible to imagine the Earl here at all. He's so full of fire and fury, surely he'd have just turned round with a snarl and gone back home to his season? There's nothing for him here. 'I think that's where my father is. The seed changed him, but not how I wanted . . . I don't know. He went there and I couldn't follow – it hurt too much. He always said I was weak.' Alberic's voice drops to a whisper and he won't look us in the eye.

'We can fix it,' I say. 'Together.'

'He never needs anyone else – except that I did this, Owl. It was my fault and when he finds out he'll be furious. I've ruined everything.'

'Well, forget him.' I grind the words out between my

teeth, and a little mist of ice breaks out on the ground around me. 'He's a mean old man and you don't need him.'

'But the world does.' Alberic finally looks up and stares at me. His eyes are dark, almost hollow. How long *has* he been here, beating himself up? 'Doesn't it? When I left to follow him, the court was already falling apart. Everybody arguing, nobody strong enough to take her on. Is it still summer?'

'We can fix it,' I urge again. 'I promise, Alberic. Just not here, not now. We need to make a plan, when we're home . . .'

'Home.' His mouth twists in a bitter smile. 'No. I'm not going back there. Not until I've fixed the mess I made.'

'Not to the court,' Mallory says. 'Everything's . . . different there. We should go back to yours, Owl. Can you magic us to your bedroom? And when we've worked out what we're doing we can come back and sort it out.'

He huffs out a hollow laugh. 'I've just told you I'm not going!'

'But you are,' Mallory says firmly. 'Come on, Owl. We're just wasting time here . . .' She grabs for Alberic and he darts away from her, but stumbles, toppling to the ground as Time rushes from the horizon towards us, a small child once more, coming closer, faster and faster. The hooded, cloaked moments join him.

'NEW THINGS!' His voice splits the air, and fat drops of rain explode on to the dry ground as she skids to a halt in front of us. 'Don't go! I haven't had new things to play with for so long, and you're all so sweet and noble for saving your friend . . . Won't you *stay*?' His voice turns to a rumble, no child's voice at all, and the clouds gather over our heads, forks of lightning dancing.

The hooded moments come, thick and fast around us. My blood spikes with fear – and with frost. We can't get stuck here now; there's nobody left to come to find us. I gather all the magic that's been building in me since we got here and thrust out my hands to stop the shifting figures. A fine mist of snow breaks out around us as they freeze on the spot. Time is the last to succumb, his small face frozen in shock, eyes wild with rage.

'Owl!' Mallory chokes, taking in the frozen figures. 'What did you do? Did you stop time? Did you *literally freeze time*? How did you do that?'

I bite my lip, turning from the frozen army to her,

my head spinning. 'Can we answer the questions later, Mallory?'

'Let's go, then,' she hisses as the ice figures behind us begin to creak. 'Quick, Owl!'

The panic floods through her voice, and we haul Alberic up between us. I close my eyes and pull on the very last reserves of my strength and will us all home, until my head is a scorching mass of wire and my knees are weak, hoping beyond hope that I get us to the right place.

By some miracle we land in the swelter of my bedroom, in a heap on the carpet. For a moment I can't see. That familiar heat is agony against my skin.

'OK?' Mallory's cool hand steadies me as I struggle to sit up. I put my back against the wall by the open window.

'It's so hot,' I whisper, looking from her to Alberic. He's huddled in the corner, watching us as if we're strangers.

'It is that,' she says. 'But at least we're in one piece. You did it, Owl!'

'Yes.' I smile. We did. We made it back home with Alberic. Mission complete. Only right now I don't feel victorious. The heat beats into me just as fiercely as it did before, and Alberic is like a husk of his former self.

He lowers his head to his knees as I stare at him. 'What are we going to do with him?' I whisper.

'When Mum and Dad said they were getting a divorce and Dad got his stupid new flat, I felt a bit like he looks now,' she says, settling down next to me. 'But it got better.'

'How?'

She shrugs. 'Little bit every day. And some days not so much.' I nod. She smiles. 'It's not easy for any of us, eh? Jack's not exactly what you hoped he'd be. We're all here now. Will your mum let him stay?'

'Yes,' I say. 'She said she'd be here, if we needed her. Hope he likes lentils.'

'Nope,' Alberic mutters into his knees.

Mallory grins. 'I'll bring some other bits later – I'd better check in at home.' She looks at me. 'You'll be all right?'

'Fine,' I say, lumbering to my feet to give her a hug. 'We got him out of there,' I whisper, worry worming in my stomach. Alberic's staring at us as though he would rather not be here, but he's just too tired to do anything about it. 'That's the main thing. We did what we needed to do . . .'

'You certainly did.' She grins, then catches my

expression. 'Freezing time will never sound the same again.'

I grimace. 'Let's hope he doesn't hold grudges.'

'So!' says Mum, looking from Alberic up to me. 'You found him! What *have* you been up to, Alberic?'

'He's been poorly – we wanted to bring him somewhere he could get some food and rest. The court is a bit under the weather at the moment, and there's nobody there to look out for him. The Earl is missing, and without him autumn can't happen, it seems. Alberic had gone to find him, but it didn't go so well . . .' My voice trails off and I take a breath, watching for her reaction.

Mum stares at me for a long moment. 'And you're caught up in this.'

I look from her to Alberic, who is just staring at us, speechless and wan with exhaustion. 'Well, yes,' I say.

'Well, yes,' she repeats, sighing, but there's a little sparkle in her eyes. She can't help her love for fae adventure, any more than I can. 'I'm glad you found him. And I can do food and rest. Did you find Jack? Is he helping you?'

I snort and she rolls her eyes.

'Let's get Alberic sorted out, then,' she says. 'He looks like he hasn't eaten in weeks!'

'He might not have,' I say. 'He got lost.' Mum stares at me for a long moment, obviously expecting more. I shrug. 'I don't really know exactly – we just got him out of there.'

'Right.' She tucks a hand under Alberic's arm and we haul him up. He is absurdly tall in my small bedroom, his skin gleaming beneath the ceiling light as he knocks into it. Mum's eyes widen, but she carries on pulling him through the room. 'Let's get him settled on the settee and I'll heat some soup. Owl, get a blanket from the cupboard, would you?'

The blanket is one we picked up over the summer, soft fleece in blue-and-white stripes. I crush it up close to my chest and inhale the comfort for a moment, remembering how easy everything seemed then. A layer of frost sweeps over the skin on my hands, and my brow tightens with it, but only for an instant. Too warm.

Too warm for Jack. Too warm for the Queen as well. Is it really only the Earl who can herald in the autumn? If we can't find him, will we be locked in this summer forever? I guess I'd hoped that bringing Alberic back would make *some* difference.

'. . . but who knows, with a boy who is half fae?' Mum is muttering to herself as I head into the cluttered sitting room. Alberic does not fit on the settee; he's propped up against one end, his legs dangling over the other, shivering despite the heat. I pile the blanket on top of him, and Mum perches on the edge, frowning. 'Owl, do you know?'

'Know what?'

'What he needs?'

'From the look of him, food.'

'I guessed that much!'

'We were told it was the human part of him that was in trouble. So I guess he needs things normal humans need . . .'

'He doesn't look very human, though,' she whispers. 'He looks like he's been stretched . . .'

'He does,' I say, peering down at him. He looks like his father, and he looks like himself, only wilder, harder, and very pale. 'I guess we should feed him. And let him sleep. There probably wasn't a lot of rest where he was.'

'I am here, y'know,' he whispers, eyes closed.

'Where were you, Alberic? Were you in one of the

fae worlds in my old book?' Mum can't help the note of excitement in her voice. She got more guarded after the adventures of last winter, but you can tell she still gets a thrill whenever anything supernatural is going on.

'He got stuck there,' I say when Alberic doesn't answer. 'We had to pull him away. He'd gone to find the Earl of October and he didn't want to leave without him.'

'Where's the Earl now? Shouldn't we call him?'

'I don't know,' I say. 'We didn't see him. I don't think you can just call him anyway, Mum. Bit like trying to call Jack . . .'

She frowns at that. She always used to talk about Jack with a hush of magic in her voice, but this summer it's got tired; she's as fed up with him as I am.

'And about as much use, I suppose,' she says.

'I couldn't find him,' says Alberic. He frowns at us, and sits up. 'Owl? What did you do? We need to go back!'

'No, you don't,' says Mum, tucking the blanket in around him. 'Stay a while, and have something to eat. Nobody's going anywhere right now.' She gives me a hard stare out of the corner of her eye. 'Where were you all?'

'We went to Time,' I say.

There's a long silence. 'I wonder what they'd say about *that* on the parenting forums,' she says eventually, looking from me to Alberic.

'We saved his life.'

'But were *you* safe? How did you even get there? Or back? What's it like?' She rocks back on her heels, and sits cross-legged on the carpet, staring at me round-eyed. 'Tell me, Owl.'

'We used the incantation,' I say. 'Mallory remembered it. To start with, it didn't work, so we went to the court and leaned on the Green Man, which helped. It feels a bit like going through a washing machine.'

'A washing machine,' she mutters. 'Definitely not recommended.'

I smile. 'And then we were there, and Father Time was there. He plays with time, all around, so the whole world keeps changing. Towers and mountains rising and falling in seconds. The ground shakes and the sky constantly shifts; sometimes storms, sometimes stars.'

'Beautiful?'

'Terrible,' says Alberic. 'I tricked my father into going there. I planted a seed on him and it was supposed to change his heart. Stupid. But I wanted him to stop being angry; to be different. Instead, he just went chasing off into Time! And I couldn't find him, so he's still there.'

'But we can't go back now,' I say.

'Why not? You did it once!'

'It took everything I had, and the Green Man's help, to get us there. And all of my magic to get us home again. It's not happening today, Alberic.'

'It certainly isn't,' Mum says, with a heavy sigh. 'Questionable whether you should *ever* try that again.'

Alberic looks from me to her, and it really is very hard to argue with my mother. She gestures for me to follow her into the kitchen, where she heats carrot soup and I cut thick wedges of the heavy rye bread she made, spreading it with a lot of butter. We don't speak and I can tell she's trying not to say a lot of things, which I appreciate, because I don't know what to say back. Alberic is a mess, and so am I – being half fae isn't exactly working out brilliantly for either of us right now. We bring the food into the sitting room on an old wooden tray carved with winter's wolves, and Alberic's eyes flash with copper as Mum puts it in front of him. He doesn't bother with a spoon, just drinks the whole lot from the bowl before mopping the sides with bread.

'When *did* you last eat?' I ask.

Alberic stares from Mum to me. 'Thanks for the soup,' he says in a low voice.

'You are welcome.' She smiles. 'There's more – I'll leave Owl to sort it out for you. I'm going to take the rest of mine upstairs – I've got some work to do. OK? We'll talk another time, Owl.'

I nod, and watch her head up the wooden steps to the attic, expertly balancing her own tray on one hand to open the door.

'So?' I ask once the door is shut behind her, leaning forward in my chair. 'What *did* happen, Alberic? You were gone for so long!'

'D'we have to do this now?' he asks.

'I just want to understand . . .'

But even as I say it he's turning ashen. The bowl spins as he lets it fall with a clatter to the floor.

'Alberic?'

'What's wrong with me?' he whispers.

'You're just tired,' I say, stooping to pick up the bowl. 'Anybody would be – you got trapped there for so long . . . I'm sorry I hassled you. Rest now, we'll talk later.'

'Need to find him.'

'We will,' I say. 'I promise.'

I clear the bowl away and then I don't know what to do with myself, so I curl up in the chair next to him, in case he wakes up.

13

'Owl?'

It's dark, and starlight filters through the open window. My neck is stiff, my mouth dry. I stir and the events of the day come back to me. I turn to Alberic and it's a relief to see him looking more alert.

'Hey,' I manage.

'Did I say thank you? I don't remember . . .'

'It doesn't matter,' I yawn. 'Do you need anything? I'm going to get water.'

'Water's good,' he says.

When I get back with tinkling glasses of iced water, he's sitting cross-legged on the floor, looking out at the stars.

'Thank you,' he says, taking one of the glasses.

'Do you want to talk about it?'

'The Earl never forgave me,' he says, taking a long drink. 'It was always difficult between us, and after I challenged him in front of the court last winter, with everyone watching, he turned against me even more. He was furious that I'd dared to argue with him, that I'd taken Jack's side. Everyone else was nice about it, but he could barely look me in the eye.

'I started to regret doing it. I went to see the Queen of May to ask her what I could do to change it. To change his opinion of me. He always thought I was weak, being half human. Jack never seemed to think the same of you . . . and you aren't weak! He was interested in you, saw you as something new and amazing, I could tell. All your frosty adventures – I'd never seen Jack like that before.' He shrugs. 'Of course you *were* new to him – he never knew you existed. Whereas my father had been stuck with me since my mum died, when I was only two. I wanted him to see me the way Jack saw you, I suppose. It sounds stupid when I say it out loud.'

'It doesn't,' I say. 'I didn't realize it made you feel that way. *I* never thought Jack found me exciting. I was more like a novelty, a bit of a joke. He never really even believed he was my father.'

'I think he did . . .'

I stare at the wood floor. It has scuff marks from where we've moved furniture over the years and the old rag rug has been bleached pale in the sun.

'He never said so. And I'd dreamed for so long of having a father, what that would be like. I definitely didn't expect him!'

'No,' says Alberic. 'I get that. He's annoying.' He smirks, and I laugh. 'But he does love you, Owl. In his way.'

'You don't think the Earl loves you?' My heart aches. Bad enough having Jack for a father, but having the Earl, and no mother either – I can't even imagine that. 'Surely . . .'

He shakes his head. 'I don't know. I just know that when he looks at me his eyes aren't happy with what they see. So I thought maybe I could make myself stronger, make him see me differently – I don't know. I've never known how to make him happy. And the Queen could see *I* was unhappy, so she offered me a seed, said it would change everything. Of course I knew there were risks, but I didn't care. I just couldn't carry on living in the court with him judging me.

'I planted the seed on him, one night at the start of summer. It was the holidays and I'd had this stupid idea that maybe we'd do something normal.' He laughs, shaking his head. 'The Earl of October, on the beach? At the park? What was I thinking . . . I planted the seed and straight away he started muttering something about the mistakes of the past, and Time. And then he vanished. I waited for ages but he never came back, and as the summer dragged on, I realized it was my fault autumn wasn't coming. I tried to make it happen myself, but I couldn't. So I went to find him . . . but it's a nightmare, that place. It's forbidden to go there, and now I know why.'

'It's forbidden?'

'To mess with time. It's one of Mother Earth's only rules. She and Father Time don't see eye to eye; she says it's best left alone. What's done is done, and what's yet to come is still a mystery.'

'But that's where the Earl went?'

'As far as I could guess,' he says. 'I couldn't find him, though I searched everywhere. And then I got lost with all those horrible moment-people, who flash in and out and don't really know anything, and the chaos.'

'I'm sorry we didn't come sooner.'

'I need to get back there – I need to find him, Owl. I don't know what he's up to. I never thought he'd leave his season. Something's gone terribly wrong – with him, and everything else! This heat is my doing. I did try to make autumn come, before I left to find him, but it was hopeless. Without him here, I don't have any power at all. And if we don't fix it now the whole world's going to be destroyed!'

'We'll fix it,' I say. 'Maybe we don't need them, Alberic. If I can use my power without Jack around, like I did in Time, then you can use yours without the Earl. Maybe you *can* bring autumn yourself!'

He laughs bitterly. 'I told you: I tried. He's the Earl of October – he *is* autumn. Just like Jack is winter. We can't compete with that! Even if you can use your power, it's hardly the same. What you did to Father Time . . .'

'I didn't mean to freeze things like that.' I wince. 'I've not been able to freeze anything properly for ages. It was cooler there and I could feel my magic coming back. And I needed to get you out. Did your magic not work?'

'I could feel it,' he says. 'To start with, I used it to search for the Earl. Then I just used it to keep myself sane. I didn't think about coming back; I didn't want to come back without him. Time'll be furious when he thaws,' Alberic says, with a shadow of a smile. 'Which will probably mean trouble later. He's a monster, Owl. So many of the fae are.'

'Monsters?'

'You don't think Jack is? That the Earl is?'

'Well, they're not always what you'd hope for . . .'

'Exactly. That's what we'll be, Owl. You remember last winter, when you were so keen to find out all the fae secrets – do you really think you're better off now that you know everything?'

'Yes!'

He shrugs, exasperated. 'I'm not sure I am. I wish I'd had a chance just to be normal.'

'I was never normal, Alberic. I just didn't know what I was. Do you really think you're so bad?'

'Potentially,' he says. 'If I allow myself to be like him. He's cruel, and cold, and he uses his power in ways he shouldn't. He's an elemental, a whole season, and he's so full of *spite*. He doesn't really care about the world – he just wants everything his own way.'

I frown. Is this why Alberic doesn't use his powers? Because he doesn't want to be like the Earl?

'You wouldn't be like him, you know,' I say.

'Really?' He looks down at one arm, elongated and

shadowed, the wrist almost like knotted wood. Like the Earl's limbs.

'Not in the important ways.'

'Not in any ways, if I can help it,' he says. 'But we need him back anyway.'

'Maybe,' I say. 'But I really think we can spare a day or two just to get you better and make a plan.'

'When did you get so sensible?' he demands in an irritated tone, flopping back into the cushions.

'When my friend went missing,' I say. 'And I'd been too preoccupied to know that he needed my help.' I get up and take our glasses to the kitchen, refilling them.

'It wasn't your fault,' he calls out.

I raid the freezer for ice and fill glasses with cold water, staring at my reflection in the window. Frost sweeps up into my hair, and my skin gleams blue, just for an instant. I wish I could believe him, but I don't. He was the first person I trusted from the world of fae. He was the one who cautioned me when I first met Jack and got so caught up in my new nature. He was the one who came with me to Jack's own world, putting himself in danger. I should have taken more care of him. Of our friendship. Maybe I'm more like Jack than I like to admit. Because, as much as this is all terrible, somewhere deep inside, I'm *glad* there's an adventure happening. I'm glad there's more than just school, and rye bread.

I'm glad I froze Time, and brought my friend back. If only he could be glad of it too.

14

All day, since we got back with Alberic, the need to see Jack has been growing. He's not in this world, obviously, and if they're all trapped, as the Queen of May said they were, then it makes sense that he's trapped in his world of winter. I've been telling myself that he doesn't want me there, and feeling all twisted and cross about it, but after our adventures in Time I just really need to see him. I remember how magical Jack's world felt. Cold, and barren, but so beautiful. And so full of his magic – our magic. I want to be there again, to feel that boom of power in the air. But more importantly I want to talk to him. I want to look him in the eye and see what Alberic says he saw. That he's proud of me. Happy that I'm in the world. Happy to be my father

So I'm trying to get to his world, right now. I

haven't got the book and I haven't got the words that Mallory and Alberic recited. Instead, I have my feet in a bucket of icy water and a stubborn determination to find him. And just a tiny shred of the power I felt when I was in Time, still lingering just beneath my skin.

'Stop, Owl,' says a female voice as I push against the heat of the evening, conjuring up images of the wolves of winter in my mind, feeling the tiniest shred of magic deep in my belly and pulling on it. 'Stop.'

'I want to talk to him. He needs to know.'

'He does know. He just can't do anything about it.'

'But why not? Doesn't he care?' I open my eyes and stare at the wooden owl on the bedpost, glowering, swishing my feet through the ice cubes in the water. She blinks her eyes and I know it's Mother Earth. Last year, when everything went so wrong, she was the one who helped us back, after our adventures in Jack's world. She intervened reluctantly – says she cannot watch every move the fae make, when the human world is her concern, but I knew then that we had a connection. Mum saw an owl when she was in Jack Frost's world and I think that's why she gave me such a ridiculous name.

'Oh, he cares,' she says. 'Here, I'll show you . . . Close your eyes . . .'

I close my eyes, and immediately I can feel the swell of winter around me. The cold, crisp air, the flurry of snow. The ice that crunches and cracks beneath my feet. But it's a dream version, a not-really-there version. Everything's muffled, and faded out.

'I want to *actually* go,' I say, irritated when my voice sounds like the whine of a toddler.

'This is as close as you can get without hurting yourself.'

Suddenly Mother Earth herself is beside me, instantly recognizable though I've only seen her once before. Her grey hair is bound into a thick plait that drops all the way down her back, and she is smaller than me, but the air rings like a bell around her, which makes staring at her very difficult.

'Hello, little Owl,' she says. 'How you've missed him . . .'

'I missed him before I knew him,' I say with a shrug. 'It's not so different.'

'But now it is bitter, because he knows you. And you think he doesn't care. Look, little Owl. Look at his fury now.'

We are treading over black ice, and it makes tiny darting sounds with every step, and the mountains are trembling, snow creeping from the peaks to gather speed and fall with a BOOM on to the icy ground.

Jack is climbing. Roaring, climbing. But he never gets anywhere. The snow sweeps him from his feet and he tumbles to the hard ice on the lake, picking himself up to start again. The wolves are howling from the black wood forest behind him and it sounds like fury.

Jack's fury.

'Why won't you let him out?'

'This is not his battle,' Mother Earth says. She takes my hands in hers and her golden eyes thunder into me. 'This is yours and it is Alberic's. This is the battle for humanity. I do not want these elemental wars to continue. Every year there is drama, every year they vie for what they should not have. I have shut the gateways, to all but you and Alberic. You are the ones who can make the difference this time – to balance the fae and the human world – and that is as it should be.'

'I don't understand!' I howl, wishing I could join Jack. Wishing he could see me. His black hair is tipped with ice, his eyes cold as lightning, and he roars once more as he lands with a smack on to the lake. The

132

shatter spreads around him and out, until the whole lake is a broken mirror, reflecting the pale, snow-filled sky.

I've missed him.

'Please,' I say, and my throat swells with tears that I don't want to cry in front of her. 'Why aren't you helping? You did last time. You saw the world was in danger and you helped us. Why is this different? What's the point of you, if you won't *do* anything?'

'You and Alberic must do this together,' she says, her voice hard, her eyes glittering. 'Alberic is drowning and he has been for too long. I need you both strong. You are all right, Owl. You have pain, and it fuels you. He has pain; he has lost his mother, and his father is a fool. He has forgotten that there are other things, that he has his own power. And you do *have* Jokul, even if it doesn't feel like it. Alberic refuses his power because it is tied to the Earl, and he does not want to be like him. That must be dealt with. You are both powerful creatures and the world needs you: your humanity, and your fae legacy, together.'

'I don't know what that means!' I say as Jack turns, wild-eyed, and Mother Earth's voice trembles.

'Alberic must find his own power.'

'And you'll let summer go on until he does? What about the rest of the world?'

'If I save it now, it will falter later,' she says. 'You and Alberic have much to do and you cannot do it without faith in yourselves and each other. He has none and needs to find it. Start at the court, little Owl. The answers are there.'

With that, she takes my arm and the world spins. I groan when I open my eyes, seasick and light-headed.

It was a dream.

But not only a dream.

He cares.

And now I know what we're fighting for.

15

Morning comes with a beat of sun on the window, blazing through the thin curtains. I slide from tangled sheets on to the floor, grateful for an instant of cool.

'This is unbearable,' I mutter to nobody, spreading myself into a star shape on the old rug, watching the digital minutes pass on the alarm clock. I should be getting ready for school; I just can't make myself move. I study my hands for a moment, willing them to find ice, but what would normally be sparkling veins on the back of my hands are more like slug trails.

'Eugh.'

Mum starts hammering on the door.

'Owww-ll! Time to get up!'

'I'm up!'

'I'll do eggs,' Mum says through the door. 'Alberic's

looking better already. Is Mallory calling for you this morning?'

'I think so!' I shout, pulling bits of uniform off the back of my chair, muttering under my breath about legacies and battles for humanity. What did Mother Earth mean by it all? She speaks just like all the other fae: in riddles and pretty, persuasive words that disintegrate to nothing as soon as they're gone. 'Do we have any clean socks?'

'In the airing cupboard!'

I open the door and hustle to the shower, spending as long as I can under the cold water, running over everything that's happened, absently making ice patterns on the shower door. They splinter and melt as soon as they're made, which seems about right. If there is power in me, it is fleeting and nonsensical – I really can't see how *we're* going to fix the world between us, me and Alberic. Even with Mallory on the case.

Alberic is still unreasonably tall, and whip-slender, but his skin no longer resembles that of a silver birch and there's colour in his cheeks.

'Morning,' he says when I bumble in, pulling my fingers through my hair. He's sitting at the kitchen table, looking a little shell-shocked, while Mum flits about with pans and dishes.

'Salt,' she mutters. 'A body needs salt.' She grabs a large pinch from the wooden bowl by the oven and sprinkles it in. 'And some milk . . .' A splash that lands half in the pan, and half on the hob. 'And butter!'

'Morning,' I say, grabbing juice from the fridge and a couple of glasses from the shelf, before sitting next to him. 'Did you sleep well?

'Yes!' He lowers his voice and leans into me. 'Does she always do this?'

'Eggs? No, it's special for you. She's feeding you up.'

'I mean, with the . . .' He flaps his hands around. 'All the movement.'

'Oh, yes.'

I get up again with a scrape of the chair, and pull knives and forks from the drawer while she swishes around me, humming.

'You do it too!' he says when I've sat down again.

'What? Get things out?'

'There's a way you both do it . . .' He shakes his head. 'I don't know. I guess it's normal for you. Thank you, for doing what you did.' He lowers his voice. 'I do feel better, though we have to get back there as soon as we can. I can't make autumn happen without him.'

'We will,' I say. 'I'll talk to Mallory today, and we can go to the court, as soon as you're feeling better . . .'

He frowns. 'I'm fine! We don't have time to sit around here!'

'What's going on?' asks Mum, turning to us.

'I don't have my uniform,' he says.

'Don't need it,' Mum says, swiping butter on to toast before adding scrambled eggs.

'I don't?' He blinks.

'Alberic, you need to rest,' I say, an image of his uniform hanging on the silver hook by the bed in the little wooden house going through my head. Would it even fit him now? 'You're not looking quite yourself, you know. And don't go back to the court yet, not without me and Mallory.'

'But I . . .'

'One day,' Mum says, sailing the plates over the table to us and turning to get her own. 'One day of blankets and rubbish telly, and biscuits. Then maybe you'll be ready to go.'

He turns from her to me, his face wide with surprise. I think of his little treehouse home, nestled in the heart of the Green Man, and wonder if he's ever watched telly before. If he's ever eaten scrambled eggs on toast.

'*One day*,' I mouth at him, pleading. 'Promise me you won't go back there alone, Alberic.'

'You can't really stop me,' he says, but it comes out more like a question than a statement.

Mum smiles, grinding pepper over her eggs. 'You'd be surprised, Alberic. Owl, why do *you* look so tired?'

'I'm fine,' I say. 'I had some weird dreams.'

She gives me a long look. I shrug. I'm not quite sure where I'd start, even if I wanted to tell her everything. Fortunately I'm saved from further scrutiny by Mallory's arrival.

'Gotta go,' I say as soon as the bell rings.

'Doesn't she want to come in?' Mum asks.

'Running late,' I say, jamming my book into my bag and making for the door. 'See you later . . .'

'Have a good day!' She bolts up and squashes a kiss on to my cheek. 'I'll be out later – I've got a workshop at uni. You'll be OK to get yourself and Alberic some tea? There's stuff in the freezer . . .' She looks at it a bit doubtfully.

'We'll find something.'

'I'm expecting you both to be here when I get in, Owl.'

139

'We will be.' I give Alberic a wave; he looks a bit worried. She is quite a lot to handle. 'Hope you both have a good day too. It will work out, Alberic, I promise. Trust me?'

He glowers at me, and I feel a little like Jack, capering around, demanding more trust than a person can possibly reasonably expect. I grin, and leave him in Mum's care and crash straight into Mallory at the top of the stairs.

'Ag, Owl!' she protests, catching herself on the railing.

'Sorry!'

'Are we in a rush?' She looks at her phone. 'We're not late. What's wrong?'

'Nothing. Just trying to get away from Mum before she reads me like a book.'

'I wanted to check in on Alberic . . .'

'He already looks better than last night. Mum persuaded him to have a day of bad telly, which will either help or kill him off entirely. Come back with me after school and we can check on him, and work out what to do next?'

'Ugh, school,' she complains. 'We should all have taken a day off. Not that Mum would've let me.'

'Was everything all right when you got home last night?'

'Yes. I told her we were studying – I made something up about history, and how time changes everything . . .' She grins.

'He wants to go back, Mallory. For the Earl.'

She sighs. 'Yes. Shame we can't just leave him there though, isn't it? Can't we help Alberic to bring autumn without him? He does have his power, so why doesn't he use it for that? Like, you managed a bit back in the court – shouldn't he be able to do that, and even a bit more, being autumn, which is next in line, as it were?'

I tell Mallory about my not-dream with Mother Earth last night, and what she was saying begins to make sense. Alberic needs to release his own power. It's all tied in with the Earl and that's why he needs to go back for him – so that he can be rid of this guilt. Also, one way or another, we need to bring autumn as soon as we can – Lady Midday's sweltering summer shows no sign of burning itself out. Even as Mallory and I talk, little darts of light speckle the corners of my vision, and it's a relief to head into the corridors of school.

'Are you OK?' Mallory asks as I stumble into her.

'I think so. Probably just yesterday catching up with me . . .'

'It was a big day,' she says, frowning at me.

'I'm fine,' I say. 'Just a bit tired.'

'You need to drink lots of water,' she says. 'And I've got some of Mum's lemon cake – that will help.'

At lunchtime, when I'm so weary I can hardly be bothered to open my lunchbox – complete with special ice pack – the cake does help. Mallory helps too, by sitting with me and bossing me through, just like the old days.

'It's good to have an adventure on the go with you,' she says, getting out a foil package of squashy cake and shoving at me to take some. 'I mean, I know it's not exactly ideal, but we've got this, Owl.'

'We've got it.' I nod absently, putting my head on my folded arms. A lovely calm silence falls over me and there's even a wisp of cool air.

'Holy moly,' says Mallory then in a hushed voice.

'Whatisit?' I mutter, distracted by the kaleidoscope patterns unfurling behind my eyelids. Maybe if I just had five minutes of sleep . . .

'Autumn just arrived in the dining hall, wearing his school uniform!'

'What?' I look up, to see Alberic stalking towards us, every bit the Earl's son, in a too-small blazer and too-short trousers. The whole room has stopped talking, and everyone is staring at him.

'Hey,' he says with a half-smile, dropping into the chair opposite us, immediately dwarfing the whole table. 'I thought I'd make an appearance – I was bored of the telethingy. And I need to know how you got to Time . . .'

16

'We told you to have a duvet day!' Mallory splutters as Alberic takes a piece of cake with long fingers, cramming it into his mouth.

'Phlumb,' he says, shaking his head.

'Pardon you?'

He swallows, and stares at us both. 'I've decided I won't be doing so much of what other people tell me any more. If you could just tell me how you managed to get to Time, I'll be off.'

Mallory snaps her mouth shut, and gives me a sideways look.

It's good to see a spark in his eyes again. Reminds me of the old Alberic, who could be a pain but knew what he was doing – most of the time. However, if he thinks we'll be letting him go alone . . .

'What's the plan, then?' I ask. 'How did you get in last time?'

'I followed after him,' he says. 'He barged through like an old elephant, and the air warped after he'd gone, so it was easy. A lot easier than it will be now, from what you've said. But you managed it once, and so I'm sure we can do it again. I'm going to find him, and fix this incessant summer,' he says. 'I've just been to the court to try and get back that way, but it's lost. The air just got thicker and those horrific plants are poisonous – I had to get out of there!' He shows us the insides of his arms, swollen and red.

'That happened to Owl too,' Mallory says. 'You're both allergic.'

'To summer,' I say with a nod. 'Which makes sense.'

'So how did you get to Time?'

'We used the incantation, with a little bit of power from the Green Man.'

'You woke him up? I couldn't get anything out of him.'

'Well, we held on to him and said the words, and it worked.'

'So let's try that again. There's no time to lose – we need to get the Earl and sort this out, now,' he says.

'OK,' Mallory says, biting her lip. 'Or . . . you could give autumn another try?'

'No,' he says. 'I'm not him. I never will be.'

I take a slow breath, staring between them. 'You never would be, Alberic. Even if you had all his power, you'd never—'

'Well, we'll never know,' he says as the bell sounds for end of lunch. 'Because we'll be bringing him back to sort it out. I'm ready to face Time. I've already battled my way back into school – they seemed to have forgotten I even go here – so I'm sure I can do this too.'

The light in his eyes wavers, just for a second, and I realize it's mostly just bravado. He's decided to fight. He's just not sure he'll win.

'What changed, Alberic?' I ask in a low tone, heading for maths after we say goodbye to Mallory. 'You've got a bit of your power back – I could feel it in the breeze in there.'

'You came for me,' he says. 'And then . . . I was at your flat this morning, and I realized I never had that. The Earl never gave me a home. I made my own home, and it wasn't perfect, but it was all right. And now Lady Midday's nearly killed the whole place – it was almost impossible to get through all her poisonous new plants, and for what? Just to flex her power? Autumn's sprites and fairies should be in there now, working with the spiders, turning the leaves gold. The Green Man should be shedding his crown, the Lady of the Lake should be grumbling about all his leaves drifting into the water – and none of them are there! They're all hiding away from Lady Midday. I managed to get into my place, the home I made with the Green Man's help, and some of the sprites. And now it's dying, because I was angry with my father. This is my mess, Owl. I have to tidy it up myself. I know what I'm doing now.'

'Do you?' I ask. 'What's going to be different?'

'I am,' he says. A tiny golden leaf flashes in his hair, and I frown. How is he doing this? What *did* change? 'I didn't know what I was doing before. Now I've seen it. You and Mallory. Your mum. The court. I forgot what I had, I was so determined to win his approval . . . I don't need him for me. I just need the court back the way it was.'

'OK. But we're coming with you. There's no way you're doing it alone.'

He grins. 'Do you think you can stop me?'

'Oh, you're just as bad as the Earl, as any of them, with your stubbornness,' I burst out, striding past him into the classroom, my heart pounding. My brain goes into overdrive, battling between being glad to have him back and looking strong again and afraid of what he's about to do. I'm angry with him, for being so dismissive of everything that just happened. He was stuck in Time for weeks – there's no *way* I'm letting that happen again. If only we'd got the Earl back with him so that we could go back to being ordinary kids. But we never were, I remind myself.

'I'll fight you,' I whisper as he sits at the desk beside mine, his knees up by his elbows in his suddenly-tiny chair. 'Just so you know. If you think you've got all powerful and sure about everything, that's great, but you're not the only one who has a stake in this. We all do.'

He stares at me and I stick out my tongue, which is very immature, but about all I can manage right now.

'You really need the book,' I tell him after school. As soon as the bell rings, he's pestering me to tell him how to get back to Time. And I know the book isn't very likely to show him anything, but it will stall him for a bit, and keep him with us. 'Unless you remember the incantation?'

Mallory shoots me a puzzled look, but for once says nothing.

'It was a year ago –' he shakes his head – 'when I was with you.'

'And you don't remember how the Earl did it?' I ask.

'I followed him,' he says. 'He didn't need any words. He just used his own power, and I sort of plunged in after.' He frowns. 'I tried this morning, but I'm nowhere near as powerful as he is, and I didn't remember the words, so nothing happened – that's why I came to find you. I suppose we might need that incantation – I'll come back with you and get it.'

'Fine,' I say, not knowing quite what we're heading into. What's he going to do when he realizes the book won't help? We needed the power of the Green Man last time, so even if Mallory still remembers the incantation – and her eyes are sparking with telling me she does – we'll not be able to do it in the flat. And I'm not so sure I'm going to be that much use right now. The walk home is brutal, and as I let us into the flat I realize there will be no relief here. Even with the curtains drawn and windows cranked open, it's like a furnace. Like all the heat in the world decided this was the good place to be.

'You look exhausted,' Alberic says with a frown as I flop into the nearest chair. 'We need to crack on, Owl, before you evaporate completely.'

'It's hot out there,' Mallory says, heading into the kitchen and coming back with water.

'I'm fine – I just need a minute,' I say as Mallory hands me a glass. 'Thanks, Mall.'

I drink deeply and let my head drop back on to the cushions. They're hot, and itchy. Just like everything else.

'So, where's the book?' asks Alberic after a while, his knees doing a little jig that makes the whole settee vibrate. He's trying to look patient and failing dismally. He looks better, at least.

'Yes,' I say, pulling myself up and stretching. 'The book . . .'

When I go to pull it out of the bottom shelf, I can feel immediately that it's still not going to be any help. If anything, it's more changed than before: lighter and smoother to the touch. The lettering on the cover is so faded it's barely legible. *Fablef and Earth-Fpiritf: How to* is all that remains, the bright gold turned to dull flecks.

'The famous book,' Alberic breathes as I sit next to

150

him and Mallory and push it on to the table.

'I'm not sure it's going to help,' I say with an exaggerated sigh.

'Oh no, the pages are blank!' Mallory says in a completely unnatural voice. I roll my eyes at her, knowing full well that she can probably see the words on the pages, even if I can't. Fortunately, Alberic doesn't seem to notice.

'What's wrong with it?' he asks, reaching out to it and flicking through a few pages. 'Not a single word!'

'Nope. We're going to have to go back to the court again,' I whisper, and this was my plan all along.

'Back home, then,' says Alberic with a sigh. 'And no incantation.' He stands, and in the glow of dusk he is a golden thing, tall and determined.

Maybe he'll do it this time. Get to Time, find his father, bring autumn home to us all. He looks like he could. But there's a darkness beneath his eyes, and it was only yesterday that he was falling apart.

'Alberic, we're coming with you,' Mallory says quietly.

'I told you I wanted to do this alone,' he says.

'But it isn't about what you want. It isn't just about you. I don't trust you both to go without me; you need a little common sense with you.'

I gape at her. 'Mallory!'

'This is my adventure too,' she says. 'And I'm the one who remembers the incantation, so you're both stuck without me.'

'You remember it?' Alberic says. 'So why are we here then, looking in the blank book? Let's go!'

'Hang on a minute,' I say. 'I need to leave Mum a note. What'll I say?'

'Tell her we've gone to the cinema to cheer up Alberic. She'll like that,' says Mallory.

'*I'd* like that,' I grumble. 'The cinema will have nice cold air conditioning, and popcorn. Now we're probably going to have to deal with the Queen and Lady Midday and . . . Time.' I stop short, suddenly afraid. 'But I said I wouldn't lie to her any more.'

'So tell her you're off to save the world and you'll be back by ten,' says Alberic.

I stare at him, grabbing the pen and a scrap of paper, deciding to write exactly what he'd said. Hopefully we'll be back by the time she is, anyway – we are going to Time, after all.

'What shall we pack?' asks Mallory, tipping her schoolbooks out on to the table. 'A torch, some water . . . maybe some string . . .' She starts ransacking the kitchen drawers, and Alberic and I watch, bemused, until she turns and catches us at it. 'What?' she demands. 'Some of us don't have fae power and have to rely on our wits!'

'And string!' I grin.

'Maybe to tie up the Queen?' Alberic joins in.

'You Never Know,' Mallory intones, grabbing a packet of biscuits from the bread bin. 'Come on, let's do this.'

We follow her into the tropical golden heat of late afternoon and my head is still buzzing with tiredness, but it's good to all be together again. We tread over familiar ground to the very heart of town and the fae magic that lies hidden there. *This* time it's going to work.

17

The court is dark and eerie, only the audible fidget
of roots beneath the hard-packed earth show it's any
different from an old bit of woodland. It took us ages
to get through the summer wilderness to the centre of
it all, and my hands sting from the brush of the blooms.
All that's keeping me going is the knowledge that this
is the only way to get to Time and bring back the Earl.
Alberic lost some of his new shine as we walked; the
place is no more friendly to him than it is to me. In
fact, going by the whispers in the foliage, it might hate
him even more. The tiny bright embers spark in the
undergrowth – Lady Midday's sprites, who will surely
be letting her know we're here, and this time we've
got autumn with us. We're not going to get anywhere
without a fight.

Many of the native trees have fallen back, away from the lake at the centre of the court, as if they're hiding. The lake itself is hardly more than a large, dark puddle, still and stagnant. Mallory has muttered the incantation twice already and I tried to harness the power of the Green Man like last time, but nothing's happening – I must be too weak from the heat. We are stuck here and time is running out – Lady Midday is bound to appear sooner or later.

'What do we do now?' I whisper, flopping on to the wiry grass in the shade of the Green Man. The others join me and for a moment nobody seems to have any answers. I can hear small things scuttle, unseen, among the new blooms that have begun to invade the lake.

'We try again,' Alberic says, stumbling back over the rustling knee-high ferns to the towering trunk of the oldest oak in the wood. 'Here, let me do it.' And he puts his hands out. 'Hey, old man . . .' he whispers. There's nothing but a murmur of a breeze through the Green Man's vast canopy.

Alberic rests his forehead against the wrinkled bark and for a long moment it feels like the whole clearing is holding its breath. There's a song in the undercurrent – I can't make out the words or even the tune, but it's there, like a low rumble, or a whisper on the back of my neck. It's a call for help, and it's coming from Alberic. He closes his eyes and the song grows bolder. A single yellow leaf drifts to the ground and I realize Alberic's using all his power to bring the court just one step closer to autumn. The air is fractionally cooler, the scent clear and earthy.

But the Green Man doesn't wake. There's a rumble, a scratching beneath the earth that might be his roots flexing, but nothing more. The cool breath dwindles against the close heat of a full summer evening, and the song drifts away.

'I'm almost there,' Alberic says. 'There's just too much heat.'

'Let me help,' I say, joining him and resting my hands alongside his, hoping to cool the air just enough for him to start his song again.

Alberic turns back to the Green Man and says words I've never heard before in that same low hum that seems to beat through the air. My skin aches with the strain of it, and Alberic is concentrating hard. And, finally, a tiny fissure of new wrinkles rush up the massive trunk, and with a deep groan the Green Man opens his dark eyes.

'Whatisit?' he grumbles.

'I need you,' Alberic says, in that same low voice. 'I need to find the Earl, and bring autumn . . .'

'What did you do?' whispers the giant.

'I planted a seed of change.'

'Upon Sorbus?'

'I tried to take it back, but I was too late. He's gone to the world of Time.'

'Then you must find him, Alberic, before he does real harm! We are not permitted to go to Time – what's he doing there? This is big trouble indeed!'

'That's what we're trying to sort out,' I say. 'This summer is killing everything, and none of you are doing anything about it.'

'Power,' rumbles the Green Man. 'Our worlds are our power source. Mother Earth has cut us off from them – she has cut off Lady Midday. Her summer will not grow stronger if she cannot return to her own realm. Speaking of whom, you'd better hurry with this plan of yours if you don't want to be fighting her. She's in fine form . . .' His voice trails off as the air grows brighter and the Queen of May appears, blossom in her pink hair, tiny blue birds darting about her.

'Oh, this is very nice,' she says, spreading her arms

and turning. 'Well done, Alberic. Not quite enough to change the season, but there's definitely a feel of it in the air.'

'It won't last long without the Earl,' Alberic says, leaning against the Green Man. That low song is still running, like a heartbeat, through everything, but now it is a faltering thing, missing beats, growing quiet.

'No?' The Queen's smile fades as she looks at him. 'Are you sure, Alberic?'

'What do you mean?' he asks, his eyes sharp. 'We are rather busy, you know. I'm not sure we need any more of your help.'

'What is this feeling?' she demands, ignoring him and turning instead to the Green Man. 'With the boy, here. What is that?'

'What does it feel like?' he asks, sounding genuinely curious.

'An ache, on the inside,' she says. 'Most unpleasant.'

'Ah,' says the Green Man. 'That is love, for our boy here. And perhaps a little guilt, for you are the one who made all of this happen, with your seed of change.'

'Love?' She looks completely shocked. 'Guilt? Don't be absurd!'

'It's what they do,' he says. 'These children of ours –

I wonder if it's why they're here.'

'How do we resolve this?' she snarls.

'We have a plan,' I say. 'We need to get to Time. And then we can find the Earl, and bring him back.'

'That is your *plan*?' the Queen demands as the blossoms in her hair turn brown at the edges and begin to wilt. 'That is the extent of it?'

'It's an evolving plan,' says Mallory. 'The main thing is to get there, right now.'

'Not enough magic between you,' the Queen says. 'I suppose you'll want our help.'

'Haven't you done enough already?' asks the Green Man with a low rumble of disapproval. 'What were you thinking of, Maeve?'

'He came to me and he was sad. I wanted him to go away. It was a seed of change, just a small token of possibility – how was I to know he'd use it to be rid of that cantankerous old fool?'

'I didn't mean to get rid of him!' protests Alberic, but they ignore him.

'You should have known anything could happen,' says the Green Man.

'And so anything has.'

'And now others have to sort out your mess.'

'Well, they'd better do it quickly. I cannot get to my world, and this one is like a furnace,' she snaps as her little songbirds desert her and the air grows heavy with heat once again. 'How do we do this – should we hold hands?' Her face wrinkles with distaste as she looks at us all, and the Green Man makes a funny little chuckling sound. 'How did it work last time?'

'We read the incantation, and Owl took some power from the Green Man,' Mallory says. 'I'm not sure we need *you* to join in.'

'Clever little bird,' the Queen snaps. 'Not to trust so easily. Come on, then. Over here with your spell.'

We gather reluctantly about the massive trunk of the Green Man, the Queen leaning against him on one side, and us on the other, holding hands. Mallory begins to speak the familiar words, and there's a pull deep in my belly, a rush of power too vast to understand.

Then it falters, leaving a tearing feeling through my chest. Alberic stumbles and Mallory's voice trails off.

Lady Midday is here.

'Keep going!' whispers the Queen, stepping forward, keeping one hand against the trunk of the Green Man.

'What is this?' comes the smooth voice of the Lady as she prowls closer, her tiny fire imps scattering across

160

the ground around her, like embers that begin to smoke. 'I did not think that you would betray me!'

'Sister, not even I can survive an eternal summer,' says the Queen of May. 'Did you really think you would go forever unchallenged?'

'But I left shade for you,' the Lady says, her wrath simmering. 'Why are you aiding these children? They are not our kin.'

'Aren't they?' asks the Queen with a sly smile. 'I think they're proving themselves just as pesky as any fae, my dear. Anyway, it's nothing personal,' she says as Mallory continues the incantation and the power begins to build once more. 'I had a similar skirmish last winter, if you remember. And the thing is, my dear Lady, it did not work. It will not work for you – *she* will not allow it.'

'She? You mean Mother Earth?' The Lady laughs, and the lake begins to smoulder. 'Don't you know what you've done with your little seed, Maeve? Your little seed has sent that stupid Earl off to change Time itself. And once that is done Mother Earth's rule will not be absolute. Anything will be possible!'

'But not spring!' the Queen snaps, as Mallory's words gather pace and Alberic's grip tightens, the

Green Man's thunder roaring in my mind. The bright green of the Queen's own power is woven through it, like blinding flashes of light. 'I cannot wrest this season from you – I need the cool of winter. I need the world to rest before it can be born again!'

'Your little seeds are no match for me.' The Lady shakes her head, a narrow smile on her mouth. 'If *only* you had considered it all before you gave one away so foolishly. What did you think Sorbus would do? Have you forgotten, Maeve? He had only ever one love, and it was not you! That human creature of his – he'd have done anything for her. Perhaps he will yet. Now stop it, children,' she hisses, her eyes burning coals. 'Little Owl, I told you that the next time I saw you I would not be playing.'

Her form is growing, taller and wilder than ever, her skin gleaming with gold as her hair turns to fire. 'Leave off this ridiculous rhyme, at once!'

She reaches out one hand, and begins to mutter dark words of her own, but Mallory's spell is cast and fire cracks in the Lady's eyes as she realizes she's too late. The combined might of the Green Man and the Queen of May sings through my skin. Alberic's eyes glow, and the ground beneath our feet shifts, and then it drops away, and we are falling through darkness.

18

I have lost Mallory. I've have lost myself. My chest burns, and everything is darkness. Something's gone terribly wrong – this isn't how it felt last time. A rush and a tumble of water catches me in its icy swell and finally, when my mind is a perfect ringing blank, spits me out on to hard ground.

Silence. The air around me is cool, the floor a silver, glittering mirror. I gather myself and jump to a crouch. Ice spills from me, a web of it that flashes across the floor and creaks to jagged peaks. The room is wide and round, doorways lining the pale quartz walls. The ceiling is aching high, pinpricked with starlight that spangles off every surface.

This is not Time.

Where am I?

'Little Owl,' comes a voice, smooth and round as a copper bell. The Lady of the Lake is before me, standing at the head of a shocked court of underwater creatures: water sprites, frogs and newts, turtles, tiny silver fish within floating bubbles of water, and tall sentries who look human but for the gills in their necks. She wears a shifting iridescent cloak and her long silver hair falls to the floor in a shining cascade. 'What is this chaos?' She picks her way through the runnels of ice towards me, frowning.

'Where are the others? Why am I here?' I ask, standing, a blizzard of cold air escaping with my words. Frost sweeps over my skin and through my hair. The power of it rolls through my blood as winter leaches through me for the first time in too long. Tiny spinning fractals scatter about me: the relief of the cold down here is overwhelming – I can't control the ice that has been kept at bay so long.

'Others?' she demands, stepping towards me. 'Little Owl, what has happened here? Who do you speak of?'

'Alberic and Mallory. They're not here?' Did they get to Time without me? My stomach is a pit of fear as I look about the vast chamber. How did I get here? Lady Midday must have done something to the spell –

but what? And where are the others?

'No. Why are *you* here?'

'But where did they go? They were in front of me!' Fear pounds through me and my skin gets tight with ice. 'Could they have got lost?' I don't even want to imagine the alternative. I stare at the Lady.

'In the lake?'

'They must be somewhere! They were with me just now!'

'Oris, please check?' she asks one of the tall, pale creatures with gills in its neck. 'Perhaps they weren't strong enough to break through . . .'

'I'll see what I can find, my Lady Belisama,' says the sentry, heading up to the ceiling, and disappearing with a shatter of light.

'Where are we?' I ask, looking after him. 'How am I breathing underwater?'

'You aren't,' she says. 'This is a cave beneath the lake. The ceiling acts as a funnel, of sorts. Everything comes in and out that way.'

'Can I get out that way? I need to find them – something's gone wrong!'

'Not without a little help,' she says with a small smile. 'Better leave it to Oris; he's my strongest swimmer.

Perhaps, while he looks, you could explain to me what you're doing here?'

'The Earl of October is missing,' I say, still staring after Oris. I can see nothing. 'I'm not supposed to be here – we need to get to Time, to find him. But don't you already know that?' I stare at her, cold fury making my voice shake. Last winter she was a voice of reason; I trusted her, more than most. 'Why are you hiding down here? Aren't you supposed to know what's going on with everyone?'

The room dims and the sentries at the doors stand straighter. They hold long crystal rods with golden hoops at the top and wear shimmering blue robes that constantly shift. Their eyes are dark and unblinking, and all are on me.

'You are more than a little like your father.' The Lady shakes her head. 'And as for what is happening up above, I cannot fix it. My concern is for the folk down here; that is what I must fight for.'

'I thought you cared for Alberic, if nothing else,' I say. 'Weren't you the one who brought him up?'

'He was with Sorbus,' she says. 'What has happened to him?'

'He was trying to *find* the Earl, after the Queen of

May tricked him! And he got lost doing it – he could've died!' I'm so angry. No wonder Alberic doesn't want to be like his father. 'Why did you leave the Earl to look after him? Why have you all just let this happen?'

My voice rises and crashes through the room, just as the sentry returns, swimming through the air, fists clenched round the collars of Alberic and Mallory, who seem to float in his wake.

Ice splinters in my veins. They're both so still.

'What happened?' the Lady asks, rushing to them as Oris lands on the floor, lowering them next to him with a grunt.

'The barrier froze,' says Oris. 'They were trapped on the other side.'

'In ice?' she demands.

'I imagine it was that one,' he says, gesturing towards me. I frown, and turn to Mallory, who rouses and pulls herself up to sit on the cold floor. Alberic is spread-eagled, blinking. The Lady bends to him, blinking hard as she helps him to sit.

'Alberic,' she says. 'What has been going on? I knew there was trouble . . .'

'Did you?' he asks in a hollow voice.

'Where are we?' Mallory asks through pale, chattering

lips. 'What happened?' I help her up, putting my arm through hers. She's so cold.

'I'm so sorry,' I say. 'I lost you. I didn't know what was going on. It was like I was drowning – I think the water froze?'

'You Jack Frosted,' Alberic says, drawing away from the Lady's touch and pulling himself up. There's a collective gasp as he unfolds, taller and wilder-looking than ever, his hair a riot of chestnut braids and tangles, tiny red leaves nestled in deep. This place is full of magic, and we're both trying to understand it. His is beautiful, and mine . . . is dangerous. I stare at my bedraggled friends and take a step back as feathers of ice rush down my arms to my hands. Sparking, beautiful and deadly. I'm not in control of my power at all – it's as if all these months of summer have wiped out my body's memory of itself.

Mallory frowns.

'Owl, it was an accident. We're OK. Look, Alberic's even got some new leaves!'

'Have I?' he asks, staring down. 'How did that happen?'

'Magic,' says the Lady. 'Strong fae magic, and a break from the poison of that infernal summer.'

'Lady Midday did this,' I say. 'She messed up the incantation.'

Mallory looks about, her eyes widening at the sparkling underwater cave. 'And so now we're . . . Where are we?'

'You are in my court,' the Lady of the Lake says. 'And lucky to be alive, by the look of you all. I'm guessing your visit here wasn't part of the plan?'

'We were supposed to be going to Time,' I say. 'But Lady Midday interrupted the spell and we ended up here – I thought I was drowning!'

I could have killed them. I nearly killed them. Everyone's staring, and it just seems to make it worse. Ice everywhere and the air around me a blue mist, dizzy with swirling snowflakes.

'Stop it,' I hiss, taking a deep breath, even as the ground under my feet creaks with ice, and frost sweeps across the floor and up the walls in a muffled blast.

'Sorry.' I wince as the Lady raises her eyebrows, looking about her throne room in stunned silence. I'd quite like to disappear right now, but I suppose that would be too easy. I look from Mallory to Alberic, who are both just staring at me, and raise my shoulders in a shrug.

'Totally Jack,' Alberic says. 'She even has the shrug down.'

'Very cool,' agrees Mallory.

I glare at them.

Belisama laughs. She laughs and laughs and the room lights up with it, the quartz walls glowing and the ice-covered floor reflecting a million dazzling stars. The silver fish spin in their bubbles and the sprites begin to dance. A couple of the sentries carve their crystal rods through the ice on the floor, breaking it into splintered chunks.

And in all the magic of the moment, Oris and his guards sweep us out of the room, down a dark corridor to a smaller chamber. Oris's movements are easy but firm as he shows us inside and shuts the door. A key turns in the lock and we are alone in a spartan cell: Mallory, Alberic and I.

'I don't believe anything I'm seeing today,' says Mallory. 'I'm just going to sit here for a minute, if you don't mind.' She collapses on to one of the chairs, and puts her head in her hands.

'Mallory? Are you OK?'

'I am very tired, with all the drowning and the ice, and the fae magic,' she says, looking up with a wan smile. 'But really you can stop looking so tormented, Owl. I'm fine.'

'I don't know what happened,' I say, pulling up a chair next to her, and propelling Alberic into it. They both look utterly exhausted. 'I'm so sorry.'

'I don't think it was you who got us off course,' Mallory says. 'It was Lady Midday, surely.'

'Doesn't matter how we got here – we need to get

out again,' Alberic says, walking to the round window and looking out into the dense blue of the underwater with a tight little sigh. 'We're supposed to be in Time, not some underwater prison!'

'We'll sort it,' I say, anxiety prickling through my skin. I sit on my hands, trying to make sure there are no more snowstorms. I think that might be the last straw for Alberic.

'Not looking good right now, though, is it?' he says, prowling to the door and rattling the handle. 'Why'd you have to make her cross, Owl? You froze her throne room, or whatever that was! And that was *after* you locked us in ice.' He turns to me, his eyes flashing copper, hair writhing with new leaves. 'We need to get out of here – why couldn't you just control yourself? The last thing we need is some kind of Jack Frost mayhem!'

'I don't know what it's got to do with Jack,' I snap. 'It's my body's reaction at being out of the summer. It was cold in the water and everything just sort of spilt out . . . You're not looking so normal yourself right now, you know. There's a bit of the *Earl* about you.'

He winces and so do I, on the inside, instantly regretting my words.

Not that he seems to regret his.

172

We stare at each other, and tiny darts of power fizz in my belly. I breathe deep, so that they don't spill out, and I reckon he's probably doing the same, judging by the flare of his nostrils.

He *does* have just as much power as me; he just doesn't normally let it out.

'Why don't you use it?' I demand. 'If you would just own it, you might have been able to do more to bring on autumn!'

'That is my father's job,' he says stiffly. 'I am not like him.'

'You should tell your face that,' I mutter.

'Stop fighting about it,' Mallory says, looking between us with growing alarm. 'We're here now. And I'm sure . . .'

But before she can finish the door opens and the Lady of the Lake enters. Alberic bolts away from her, settling into a chair as she looks around and tuts. 'Oris is most unkind sometimes, isn't he? I didn't mean him to lock you in a cell!' She walks around the room, one hand trailing over the wall and, as she goes, the room shifts around her. The cold marble floor becomes a thick pale carpet; the chairs that Mallory and Alberic are sitting in shift around them, becoming larger and heaped with cushions. The light changes from a cold blue to golden, and finally, as she completes her circuit, a table appears in the middle of the room, laden with a steaming silver pot and plates of cakes.

'That is better,' she says, perching on the edge of a deep, silver velvet settee and drawing me down with her. 'Come. Eat and drink. You do not look well, Alberic. Where is your father?'

'He's lost in Time,' Alberic says, as Belisama pours hot chocolate from the pot into small silver cups. 'The Queen tricked me . . . I thought it might make him easier, but it went wrong . . . It's all my fault!'

'Don't be so decided upon that,' the Lady says gently.

'Well, you weren't there,' he says. The Lady flinches. 'In any case, we need to go,' he says. 'Now.'

'You cannot travel onward in the way you came here,' she says. 'Your spell was an earthly thing – it won't work here.'

Alberic stares at her, horrified. 'So then how? We have to get back there!'

'I'll help you,' she says. 'There is a way. But for now you need food, and rest. And I am not to be argued with upon that point, Alberic.' There's a new tone in her voice as she says it, and Alberic obviously knows it well; he doesn't even try.

'And so this seed sent him off to Time, and you followed him?' she presses then.

'I didn't know where we were to start with. But Time was there, with all his moments. I watched a thousand years pass, in the space of a day, but by the time I worked out what was going on it was too late – I'd lost the Earl.'

She grimaces, and motions for us all to drink. Long, silent moments are filled with the most delicious interval of hot chocolate and sweet sugary cakes.

'You were tricked,' she says eventually. 'Alberic, it's important that you hear me. The Queen of May is a trickster, more than most, and chaos is fuel for her. I doubt she had anticipated Sorbus would go off to Time. She has given Lady Midday free rein, which I'm sure she hadn't planned for, and your father was caught up in it – but he is a season. He is one of the most powerful creatures in the world. He is responsible for himself. He had power enough to fight her spell, had he wanted to. Do you understand that you are not responsible for this?'

'Yes. No.' His voice is brittle, his eyes dark with exhaustion and, though there's a flush in his cheeks from the food and drink, he looks more hollow than ever. 'I was responsible for planting the seed that led him off. I don't know why he charged into Time like that, but whatever it was has kept him there, and I'm responsible for finding him now. If I can't –' he gives me a look – 'then I will have to try to bring autumn myself.'

'That is an idea,' the Lady says. 'Have you tried, Alberic?'

'Early on, when he first went off and I could see that autumn wasn't happening as it should, I tried. It made a bit of a difference, but not enough. Lady Midday charged in and laughed at me – she said I was no match for her.'

'And you believed her?'

'She was only repeating what the Earl's said before,' he says with a frown. 'That I'm not made for it. Half human, half fae, not strong enough to make a difference in either world.'

'And you believed him.' The Lady sighs.

'I did then,' he says. 'Now I'm starting to wonder.'

'Good,' she says. 'You should. And what of you, Owl? What of Jokul?'

'He's locked in his world,' I say. 'And the heat has

sort of killed off my powers. I think that's why they spilt out here – sorry – it's the cold. It's a relief.'

She narrows her eyes at me, and my vision falters. When I can see clearly again, both Mallory and Alberic are sleeping in the comfy chairs.

'What did you do?'

'I needed to speak with you,' she says. 'What did Mother Earth say, Owl? I know you have a connection with her.'

'She said Alberic has to find the Earl, and his power. She said something about how he and I, being half human, would make the difference.'

'I don't know about that bit,' she says. 'But I do agree with her about Alberic. He must be the one to find the Earl. He will never forgive himself if he does not. But it might be that you do not need to bring Sorbus back with you, Owl.'

'What do you mean?'

'It might be that Alberic needs to bring autumn himself.'

I stare at her, and then at Alberic, who is snoring. 'He says he tried – he can't!'

'But I suspect he may be wrong,' she says. 'And that is what Mother Earth was trying to tell you, Owl.'

'She did mention it . . .'

She smiles, knowingly. 'So it is there already. The seed of an idea.'

'Seeds haven't done us many favours so far.'

'Who knows,' she says. 'Things don't happen without reason, Owl. Alberic's power will never grow while he is so encumbered by his father.'

'How does it work like that?' I demand. 'My power is all Jack's, but it's not broken without him.'

'You are you,' she says. 'Your mother raised you without Jokul. You have never relied upon him for your security, or for your identity. Alberic is tied to his father in more complicated ways and that is in part my fault. I should have done as good a job as your mother Isolde did. I am no more human than Jokul, or Sorbus.' She looks from me to Alberic, and sighs. 'But perhaps that is no reason at all. No reason for any of us not to be as caring. Perhaps that is the whole point of all this. He has your friendship at least and that is much. And you'll all need it. I have no idea what Sorbus has been up to; he has been angry for so long. Ever since he came back to the court with Alberic as a small boy, he has carried his fury like a torch. Perhaps this has been a long time coming. In any case, we must do what we can to fix it now. When Time is involved, anything is possible, including complete destruction. He is a harbinger of chaos.'

Her words are horrifying, but my eyes itch with tiredness.

'Do you think we can get him back?' I ask, my voice sounding small and far away.

'I think that between you, you are capable of much.' She smiles. Her face is smooth as marble in the golden light of the underwater palace, and she holds herself so still as she sits with her hands in her lap, watching us. She's like a statue, I think. A regal statue. Her eyes glitter and there's a slender, winking crown on her head that somehow I'd missed before. It's like tears, shed but never landing, gathered on her brow.

My hand drops the cup, and it spins in silver whorls to the floor, as everything goes dark.

20

The bed is soft and a heavy quilt has been tucked over me. Sunlight filters through a mullioned window on to the pale carpet. Tear-shaped globes hang from the ceiling on ornate chains, bubbling with golden light, and shelves line the walls, all of them rimed with ice. I squint and look more carefully around me. Fine snow glitters at the edges of the carpet, and the window is glinting with frost. The posts on the ends of the bed are thick with ice. I hold my hands up before my face and see the fine loops and whorls of frost on my skin and for a moment all is well. All is magical and Jack is about to knock at the window.

And then I remember where I am, and why.

I bolt out of bed, my bare feet crunching through tiny ice crystals nestled into the carpet, and make for the door. It's a huge relief when the handle turns. I venture out into a wide, round hall flooded with early morning light and start trying the other door handles, searching for my friends.

Mallory is in the room next to mine and her bedroom looks just as it does at home, except there are a few more photos of her parents, cheek to cheek and looking happy. She rolls over in her sleep, and starts to snore. I close the door gently and move to the next room.

Which I can barely get into.

Branches, entwined and creaking, suffused with copper, dropping autumn leaves to the floor in thick carpets of red and gold. They start at the bed and have filled the entire room in a snaking nest. Alberic is almost waxen at the centre of them. He shifts restlessly and the room darkens as branches begin to snap, pushing at the walls.

'Alberic,' I call softly, from the safety of the doorway. 'Wake up!'

He doesn't stir. On an impulse, I reach out and touch the nearest twig. Frost wraps around it and begins to spread.

'Oh dear,' I whisper as the entire room chills. 'That may have been a mistake.' The frost is quick as lightning now and it rushes to every branch, finally reaching the vast trunks at the corners of the bed.

Alberic sits up with a jolt, ice making his hair stand on end.

'OWL!' he roars.

'Sorrrry!'

'What are you doing?'

'I was trying to wake you!'

He stares at me, and then around at the room.

'Why was I asleep? Where are we? What is all this?'

'You made a forest in your sleep!' I say, remembering what the Lady of the Lake said last night. This is his power. He *does* have it; he just doesn't believe it. 'It's incredible! Look at all the leaves on the floor!'

'Don't patronize me,' he says, flumping back into the bed and pulling the covers up. 'This place is full of magic – it's not me. You've made it all freeze anyway – go away!'

'Get up, then!' I shout, flouncing out and banging the door behind me. Oris is standing in the hall, his arms folded.

'Having fun, little Owl?' he asks very politely.

I bare my teeth in a smile.

'Are we prisoners here?' I ask.

'Do these look like dungeons?'

'I don't know what underwater palace dungeons might look like,' I say.

'You are not prisoners,' he says. 'Merely guests, and shortly to be leaving.' He sounds quite relieved about that. 'Come to breakfast,' he says, gesturing down the corridor. A wash of silver bubbles dances along to a doorway in the distance. 'Bring your friends, if they're still your friends . . .'

I scowl at him as he saunters away and knock on both Mallory and Alberic's doors again, shouting at them to get up, hearing my mum's voice in my head. How much time is passing while we do this? Will she be panicking? Worry gnaws at me while I wait for my friends, but by the time they've come out of their rooms I have reasoned that probably no time has passed in the real world, and, if it has, she'll have suspected we're off on an adventure and know I'll be OK. There's a bit of a wobble there, though, because what if we aren't OK?

'Owl!' Mallory stumbles out of her room and into me. 'I'm so glad you're here. I woke up and that bedroom was just like mine at home, only it wasn't, and then I remembered where we are – what happened?'

'The Lady sent us to sleep. Or the hot chocolate did.

Do you feel rested?' I examine her and Alberic, as he comes out of his room, tripping over roots and scowling. They do indeed look about a million times better than they did last night, or whenever it was before we slept. 'There's breakfast, apparently. Are you ready?'

'Yes!' Mallory says, and we jostle each other down the corridor, following the bubbles to a vast underwater cave full of spinning blue lights and a table that groans beneath silver platters with enough food to fill an entire court's worth of sea creatures.

Which is just as well, because they're all here, sitting on broad benches by the table, staring at us.

THE MOONRAZOR

Deep in fae waters there are creatures never caught by human eyes. A myriad of them, bright as planets, stranger than the wildest imagination could invent. Shoals of glitter-skinned river babies, and eels with eyes like stars. The moonrazor is the fae who dwells the deepest. Light runs through their skin, in rainbow colours that change with their mood. And their moods are not to be underestimated, for they are capable of great rage. Their world is clotted with the stuff of humans, and the moonrazor is fierce, but it is fragile. Few are the moonrazor. Few and dwindling, and full of flickering rage.

21

'Come,' says the Lady of the Lake, rising from the head of the table and gesturing to empty seats on the benches beside her. 'Join us.'

The room is still and silent as we make our way to the head of the table. Belisama is talking to Oris, who is scowling, and many of the strange faces here look unhappy. The light of the morning is silver cold, and it glitters in the bubbles that float all around us.

'They don't like us,' Mallory whispers, folding herself on to one of the benches.

'No, they don't look very happy,' I say, keeping my head low as I join her.

'We're probably a bit human for their taste,' says Alberic.

Mallory grimaces. 'Don't they know we're on a save-the-world mission?'

'That might mean more,' comes a sibilant voice, 'if it weren't for humans destroying it in the first place.' The voice belongs to a woman sitting opposite us. Her enormous eyes are black and hard with rage, and tiny darts of green light fleck through her translucent skin. She has fins in place of arms and they constantly shift in an invisible current.

'Not *all* humans, and not all *human*, either,' the Lady says mildly. 'Do you not see who they are, Aurelia?'

'I see ice in one of them, and ghosts in another. The third is less easy to read.'

'Ghosts?' Mallory asks. 'Who has *ghosts*?'

'That one.' Aurelia gestures at Alberic. 'And you are the less easy to read.' She leans forward. 'Why is that?'

'No magic?' Mallory says.

'No fae. You do not belong here.'

'Well, we'll be leaving soon anyway,' I say as the air around me chills, setting tiny fractals spinning.

'We need to get going,' Alberic says, shifting in his seat. His jaw is set, his eyes glittering with impatience. 'There's no time for this, and I don't like to be stared at.' He glowers down the table.

'They're staring at all of us,' I say, my voice straining as I try to keep my power in check. An icy banquet scene isn't going to make us any more popular and I can feel it building behind my eyes. 'Don't be an idiot.'

'I am the idiot who got us into this mess,' he says. 'And all this sleeping and eating is just getting in the way!'

'You think you can fight the biggest battle of your life without such things?' Belisama demands. 'You speak like your father, you know.'

'He would not say so.'

'He is a bigger fool than you,' she says. 'First you eat, then we will set you on your way, with half a chance of succeeding.' Her voice is melodic, and there's a song in it that seems to filter through the room. She fixes Aurelia with a hard stare. 'Do you really blame these three children for everything the world has got wrong? With all your foresight do you not see the destiny in them? They are here because *others* have made mistakes.'

'They smell like trouble.'

'They smell of adventure,' the Lady says.

'Here,' says Oris, pushing one of the platters towards us, giving Aurelia a hard look. 'Have some of these.'

There are small, sweet buns ridged with sugar crystals,

salty strips of something that looks like a weed and tiny pale fruit that burst in my mouth and taste like spiced honey. A pot of warm, golden tea is passed around and, after a time, the Lady's song still reverberating through the room in waves, even Aurelia is less fierce.

'We need to know how to get to Time,' I say to Belisama when the voices of those around us have risen in animated conversation and laughter.

'Through the Tides,' she says, leaning forward, her eyes sparking. 'In the darkest part of the lake, where it joins the river and leads to the rapids – there you'll find the Tides. They shift and change, and Time loves them. You'll find a way through, if you're lucky.'

'And will they be lucky?' asks Oris in a mild voice, spearing a morsel with a tarnished silver fork.

'I am not in charge of that,' the Lady says. 'All I can do is set them on the right path.'

'And hope that Luck will be with them?' Aurelia says.

'Is Luck real? I mean, a real fae . . . person?' I ask.

'Oh yes,' Aurelia says, her lights flickering to purple. 'You cannot mistake her. Though you may not see her, not with your little human eyes.'

'Luck keeps her own counsel –' the Lady shrugs –

'but there are a couple of things we can do to help.'

'Must you be so involved in this human drama?' Aurelia asks. 'Don't we have enough troubles of our own down here?'

'It's all connected,' says Belisama. 'What happens in one part of the world affects every other part – you know that, Aurelia.'

'I know that I am the only one left of my kind,' Aurelia says, her lights swarming, blue and green and golden.

'That we have found! You came here for my help, and I will help you, Aurelia.'

'It was a mistake to come here – I should have known that none could search better than me. You think that sending these children to Time is going to change the world? Even if they bring back the Earl of October, whoever he is, that will not solve all of *our* problems – you are naïve if you think so.'

'Aurelia, that is enough!' snaps Belisama as the room quietens. 'I don't say that they will fix all of the world's problems. Of course they won't, not alone. But they may succeed in this first challenge to restore the seasons. And after that they will know better what the world is worth and the power they have to make change. This is the first step, hopefully towards a better world for all of us. Have you met Jokul, or the Earl of October? Elemental figures, full of pride and whimsy and so much power between them – and these children have changed everything for them already. They know what it is to love now – even if it sits uncomfortably with them. To consider the wellbeing of another; to risk losing something fragile. It changes everything – or it will, by the time this is done. And now these three will carry *your* story with them for the rest of their lives, having heard it here.'

'Will you?' demands Aurelia, staring at us. 'Will you take my story? What will you take it to mean?'

'Are you really the last of your kind?' asks Mallory in a whisper.

'That we know of,' says Belisama. 'We are still searching.'

'I'm so sorry,' says Mallory in a halting voice. 'What *are* you, exactly?'

'I am exactly a moonrazor,' says Aurelia, with a flash of her fins.

Mallory nods, and Aurelia won't know it but I've seen that look on her face before. It's a recording, assessing sort of look that takes something and doesn't let it go until it's sorted.

'Now come,' says Belisama. 'We must get you ready for your journey.'

She escorts us to a cave-like room. Water crashes against the walls, and there's a chill that expands my chest. A layer of frost spreads out from my feet across the stone floor and up the shelves that line the rough, whitewashed walls.

Treasure is here, glinting on every shelf. Heavy chains of gold, and silver – some of them tarnished. Glowing brass candlesticks, tall ceramic jugs glazed and bejewelled, glittering gems, a thousand pieces of cracked porcelain and enormous wooden chests with iron straps.

'Where did all this come from?' Mallory breathes, skirting an enormous empty marble fountain with a large stone fish at its centre.

'The water,' the Lady says. 'This is the bright side. The dark is all the plastic. We have our ways of dealing with that, but often it's too late for the creatures trapped in it . . .'

It's not like I didn't know this. But to meet Aurelia and see the evidence of it all here is crushing.

'There is still hope,' Belisama says, taking in our

expressions. 'There is always hope. For now, let's get you ready for Time. You have already been lost there too long, Alberic. You know how it takes moments from you. It can take all of you, if you're not careful. I mean to arm you.'

She walks to the shelves, and her song makes the air heavy. She pulls out boxes inlaid with mother of pearl and little marble drawers. As she walks, the room gets warmer, a golden mist unfurling around our ankles.

'This is for you,' she says to Alberic. She presses a golden leaf with tiny glittering veins into his palm and folds his fingers around it. 'Keep it close and remember who you are. Apart from your father and your sadness, remember that you are not alone. I have been with you since you were tiny; I know your heart. I know how your laughter sounds. I remember the day you fell out of the Green Man and he caught you before you hit the ground. Small moments, but enough. Keep hold of all those things, while you are there, and you'll come back to me.'

'Come back to you?' He frowns, clutching the leaf, his knuckles pale.

'Always,' she says. 'There is always a home for you here, Alberic. I'm sorry if I didn't tell you loudly enough before.'

She holds up a clear hoop on a strand of leather. 'For you, Mallory. It is made of the plastic my sentries collected under a full moon. There is power of the moon itself inside, when you are ready.'

'Thank you,' says Mallory, putting the leather strand over her head, and fingering the hoop. It's the size of a small clementine, perfectly round.

'And Owl,' says the Lady. 'The perfect thing, if I can only find it . . .' She rummages through a chest of treasure, her fine fingers untangling chains and tossing rings aside. 'Where are you . . . ah!' She holds up a pendant with a carved silver wolf's head, teeth bared, fierce as it is beautiful, and so intricate. 'This was your father's. It was made for him a long time ago, by a smith who knew the fae well. He lost it in the lake, and I kept it. It was mean of me, I suppose. I was waiting for the right day to give it back to him – perhaps this is why I've waited so long.'

She loops the chain round my neck and settles the wolf against my skin, where it freezes. I shiver, feeling the ice forming through my hair, and her eyes gleam.

'Goodness,' she says. 'No wonder there's ice everywhere. Remember, what Time intends is chaos. He brings it with panic, and loss, and great change that makes the ground shift beneath your feet. Stay true to this feeling, right here . . .'

'Thank you,' I say.

We head back to the door, trailing behind her, but when we pass the old fountain the stone fish at its centre begins to spout. Alberic stops first as the basin fills quickly with heaving, bubbling water.

'What's this?' he asks.

Belisama frowns. 'My mirror, the heart of the lake – but what *is* this?' she mutters to herself, stepping closer. Alberic is already kneeling, leaning towards the water. It stills beneath his gaze, and a scene emerges, crystal clear.

It's a darkened room in which a very small boy is huddled in blankets on a bed beside a woman. A tall, shadowed figure stoops and picks up the boy, who kicks and screams. The woman doesn't stir. The figure tucks the boy under one arm and turns to the window. It flies open and a rush of autumn leaves spins towards the pair. The boy stops struggling and reaches for one of them, grasping it in his fist.

'Leaf,' he says.

'Leaf,' agrees the figure carrying him. 'Let it go now.'

The boy lets it go and it drifts to the ground, its fluted edges now glittering with copper.

The figure pauses to look more closely at the leaf and then he vaults through the window, taking the boy with him.

'Mama!' comes a protesting voice through the window.

But the woman on the bed doesn't stir.

And now a new figure joins her, standing by the bed like an apparition. He is like the one who just left with the boy, only taller, broader, his skin greyer. Tiny leaves crown his head, and run down his trunk-like neck.

'Back,' says the Earl.

The lake dims, and then a new scene appears. It is the Earl of October in full splendour: golden-skinned and haloed with a thousand twining branches, ruby-red leaves twisting through them. He walks through woodland, his eyes glittering as the trees around him lose their leaves, and conkers thump to the ground in prickled green cases. A woman is with him – the same woman who was lying still in the bed. She has fiery red hair and when he looks down at her she nudges into him.

'I suppose you think this is impressive?' she asks.

He halts, tilting his head to one side.

'You do not think so?'

'It's the most beautiful thing I've ever seen,' she says, looking him in the eye. 'But *impressive*? Impressive is courage and endeavour. These things –' she sweeps her arm out at the clearing – 'are as impressive as it is for me to breathe. It is in your nature.'

'You think I should try harder?'

'I think you should try something new with all your power.'

'My power is autumn – it is for the world.'

'But is that all you are?'

He considers, while leaves spiral all around them.

'No,' he says. And he smiles. 'Are you ready, then, to be impressed?'

She laughs, and he puts his arm round her and lifts her to his shoulders and *runs*, while the trees throw back their arms and stars break free of the clouds. The whole world seems to move beneath his feet as he crosses rivers and vast forests to reach a single mountain, where an ancient tree sprawls, wide as a city, reaching for the sky with a million twisted branches.

The woman slips to the ground and stands with the Earl, her face wide with wonder. She reaches for the tree, running her hands over the serrated bark. The Earl touches one green leaf and its centre glows with red.

'That is amazing,' the woman says. 'It is still autumn, however.'

'Autumn is who I am!'

'And a man, Sorbus? A creature who is capable of love?'

He frowns.

'You are thinking too hard,' says the woman. 'Just do the thing that is in your heart. If you have one!'

He takes her hand in his. 'I have one,' he says. 'It just beats a little slower than yours.'

'Forward,' barks the Earl's voice, and the scene disappears. The dark room emerges and the boy is back in the bed, the woman holding him tight.

'I love you,' she says. 'Whoever you become, whatever trials you face, however you fight them, remember, I love—'

'Now!' roars the voice of the Earl.

'No!' screams the Lady of the Lake. The image falters, and disappears.

Alberic stumbles back from the fountain.

'What was that?' he whispers. 'Was that me? Was it

my mother? Why did you get rid of it?'

'He is trying to stop time,' the Lady breathes. '*That's* what he's been doing all this time; your connection with him has brought it to the surface here. You must go quickly, and stop him. I will only have disrupted him for a moment. You must go and stop him!'

'Stop him from what?'

'From stopping time. From bringing your mother back. That's what he's been doing all this time, Alberic – and it looks like he's nearly there!'

22

'What?' Alberic's voice is a hushed, horrified whisper. 'What did you just say?'

'He is trying to find the moment she died,' the Lady says, taking a steadying breath. 'He is filtering through Time; he seeks to change the moment.'

'Can he do that?' I ask, finding my voice at the end of a very long, dry tunnel. 'Lady Midday was right, Alberic. She said he'd do anything for his human creature – she meant your mum! But . . . is it possible?'

'He is in the world where anything is possible,' the Lady says.

'But how would that even work? Would she have been here all along? Will she appear now?'

'It would change every moment between.'

'Would that be so bad?' asks Alberic.

'It is against everything that we are,' the Lady says. 'It is against harmony, and the rules of the world itself.'

'Or Mother Earth's rules.'

'You think she's wrong?'

Alberic doesn't say anything.

'I don't know what would happen,' the Lady says. 'It mustn't *happen*. Owl, you see that?'

We are all speechless. How can we all stand here and deny Alberic his mother?

'We see it,' Mallory says eventually, her voice firm as we follow the Lady out of the cavern and down the mirrored corridor to the main hall. 'We'll find him. What we just saw, in the fountain . . .'

Alberic stares from her to me. 'I didn't remember,' he says. 'If that was real, then I should remember, shouldn't I? She told me to remember and I didn't.'

'You were very small,' I say.

'I never saw him like that. I don't know them at all – I never did. He blamed the human weakness in me for everything that happened, and everything I tried to do just made it worse, and there was nobody who understood and I was so *angry*. I tried to talk to him, to explain, but all my words came out wrong and made him angry too and . . . I just wanted him to get it.

When I planted that seed, it was all I wanted. I wanted to be able to really talk to him, about everything, but especially about her. We never did; he always told me he couldn't stand to be reminded – and there I was, to remind him with every moment. Any time I didn't act the way he wanted, or do the thing he expected, there it was. I reminded him of her. I didn't know it was love that he felt for her. I didn't know that the anger was because she'd gone. That whole thing about humanity and weakness was just fear.'

'We'll find him, and maybe he'll listen now,' I say.

'Or he can bring her back.'

'Let's just get there,' says Mallory. 'And we can work it out when we find him.'

We're back in the main hall of the Lady of the Lake's underwater home, the cave beneath the funnel where the lake lies still and muddy at the centre of the old fae court, and silence has consumed us all.

'Up through the barrier –' the Lady's voice breaks through the deep – 'and then you'll need to head south to the Tides, where the veil between worlds is thin. When you get there, keep your wits about you and your eyes wide – you'll find the entrance to his world.'

'This is foolish,' says Oris, folding his arms. 'If things are as serious as you have led us to believe, then why are we sending children on this mission?'

'This is their journey,' the Lady says. 'What has age to do with anything, Oris? Are you wiser now than you were when you were a child?'

'I was never a child, my Lady,' he says with a frown.

'We all were children once,' she says, firmly. 'And these ones are trusted by greater forces than us. This is their test. Now, up with you all and don't look back.' Her eyes grow mirror-fierce. 'Never look back.'

We follow Oris, then, and the Lady's court watches from below as he leads us to the barrier, where the real world waits.

'You don't want to be back in the lake,' he says in a gruff voice, looking up through the Lady of the Lake's magical barrier to the clear waters of a river. 'You'll have to swim hard, against the tide, so that you end up in the river that leads to it. Can you all swim?'

We nod and my heart hammers in my chest. What if I freeze the water again? What if one of us can't fight against the Tides? I have images in my mind of that white churn, where there is no up or down.

'When you reach the Tides, they'll carry you away.

Just keep swimming. Keep moving, and you'll get there. Luck be with you,' he says, and then he reaches up, and catches us, one by one, thrusting us into the spinning cold water. Alberic goes first, and then Mallory, and I am last, and I'm concentrating so hard on not freezing things that for a moment I panic. Until Mallory's hand reaches for me and pulls me out on to the surface of a rushing silver river.

The air is searing, the water reflecting the orange of the sky. It's sunset, wherever we are, and ahead of us is a roaring sound.

'Do you suppose that's south?' Mallory asks, peering at the horizon, where the water turns white. Alberic is still silent, treading water, his eyes distant.

'Alberic?'

'I don't know about south,' he mumbles. 'Just let me be for a minute . . .'

'That would be easier if we weren't in the middle of a freezing lake, about to take on Time!' Mallory says. 'We're in this together, Alberic.'

'You really think that?' He laughs.

'Why else would we be here?' I demand.

'You're here because I messed up, and now the whole world is wrong, and we need to make it right.

You shouldn't have come with me. You'll probably just drown and then I'll feel even worse,' he says.

'Yes, well that might suit you, but I think we'd rather not,' I say, my voice crisp. 'Mallory, try your hoop thing. It's got the power of the moon, or whatever – maybe it'll show you something we can't see.'

'Ooh, like a magical monocle. Or a compass. That'd be convenient, wouldn't it?' She holds the hoop up to one eye and peers through it. And grins. 'Well, what do you know!'

'What? What do you see?' I push myself over to her. 'Can I try?'

She passes it to me and I huddle close to look. Nothing is different.

'Well, that's not very helpful, is it?' I sigh.

'You can't see it?' She sounds utterly delighted. 'Ha! Maybe I'm good for something, after all.'

'Mallory! Whoever said you weren't?'

'Maybe it's difficult, sometimes, being best friends with a couple of magical people,' she says. 'Maybe, sometimes, I feel small and boring and unimportant.'

I goggle at her.

'You are both being very un-heroic right now,' I say. 'Shall we have this adventure? Or we could probably just swim to the shore there, and go home?'

'I said *maybe*,' Mallory says.

'I say definitely not,' I say. 'Apart from anything else, you were the one who got us to Time in the first place, to find Alberic!'

'This is true.' She nods. 'And what I saw was the Tides. They're the booming bit.'

'That makes sense,' I say. 'Shall we do it, then? Will your magical hoop act as a breathing device for when we start drowning?'

'Who knows,' she says. 'It is an all-magical hoop, after all.'

'Let's do it,' I say. 'Alberic. Are you ready?'

He looks at me as if I just woke him from a dream. 'Ready?'

'To find the Earl and bring him home. That's the plan, remember?'

Alberic sighs, and joins us as we start to swim towards the rumble of the Tides. For a moment, it is quiet. It is the three of us, no words, only the sweep of arms and push of legs. And then the current picks us up and hurls us into chaos.

Light and dark, the churn of feet overhead, and the

pounding of my heart. My breath comes in splinters and then funnels of ice as we fall with a torrent of furious water, and the weight of it when I land is crushing. I push myself forward with spaghetti arms, looking wildly for the others, reaching out for them, and then I'm swept off my feet again.

They are called the Tides for a reason. Seven times I am hurled into the watery storm. Seven times my breath is spent, my chest a tangle of ice. Seven times it is Mallory's hands that pull me through. Only, on the seventh time, it is not into the fiery night air that we emerge. It is dark and still, and mountains crumble in the distance. The shore is bleak and barren, the grey sand beneath us hard and cold.

We're back in the world of Time and, even as we struggle onwards, I can see the moments gathering: strange spectral shapes that seem to blot out the light, created by Time to live just for the blink of an eye. He'll know we're here – it's just a matter of time before we have to deal with him. And last time I froze him, so there's that to worry about. For now, though, all I can do is watch things unfold before me. A tall, slender castle rises out of a field of green grass, and the sun breaks through the clouds just for an instant, bathing the whole scene in golden light before the castle turns grey and starts to fall apart beneath a sudden fierce wind.

'Owl? Sit a minute,' Mallory whispers, pushing me forward on to a patch of grey, featureless ground that seems to be permanent – for now. Her hair is a tangle of wild dark curls, dripping on to frost-covered grass as she rushes off. Sunrise turns the sky into streaks of pink and gold, and then storm clouds begin to gather on the horizon. I sit and watch it numbly as frost grows around me, feathering over coarse ground, and then Mallory is back, pushing Alberic before her.

'Right,' she says, breathing hard as he drops to the ground beside me. 'I didn't know you were both such terrible swimmers!'

'How did you do that, Mallory?' I ask.

'The hoop,' she says. 'I could see you through it. The rest is all thanks to my dad insisting I should be able to survive a boat capsizing.'

'The cursed swimming lessons.' I smile, remembering how she used to complain when she had to get up early every Saturday morning so her dad could take her.

'The cursed swimming lessons.' She grins. 'So here we are. Where do you suppose Time is hiding, then?'

'We're hoping he'll stay away, aren't we?' I ask.

'Well, that doesn't mean anything,' she says. 'I hoped for a pony when I was five. I guess we'll just keep our eyes out – he's not exactly subtle, is he? Any clues for what we should do now? Alberic?'

He shakes his head, shivering. He looks freezing, and a little bit like he's reliving his worst nightmare, which he probably is right now. Last time he was here, lost, for weeks. I try to pull back my frost, but it's bursting all over my skin in tiny crystals.

'Frosty power likes it here,' Mallory says. 'What about autumn?'

'No,' he says.

'Alberic?'

'Nothing,' he says. His eyes glow. 'I was on such a mission. I was so sure that I was going to find him and have it out with him and then make autumn happen. Now I don't know any more. If he's really gone back in time to save her . . .'

'Maybe he has,' I say. 'But that doesn't mean it can be done, Alberic.'

'But if he stops time . . . if he changes it, then it could be real.'

'But it wasn't,' says Mallory. 'It isn't real, because

it isn't what happened. You wouldn't be you; nothing would be as it is.' She pulls her rucksack round and digs into it, finding a packet of soggy biscuits.

'What's the harm in that, though?' he demands, taking one from her absently. 'Really. Would the world implode just because one woman doesn't die?'

'Let's find him first,' I say. And I'm hoping that a miracle will happen along the way that will make it all make sense, because I don't know the answer and neither does Mallory. I take a bite of one of her biscuits, and it doesn't taste nearly as bad as it should. A little wriggle of warmth worms through me. Why shouldn't the world give him that? Would it really be so wrong?

'I guess so,' says Alberic, taking a deep breath and scrambling up. 'It's impossible to get your bearings here – everything changes constantly. Do you think your magical hoop will find him, Mallory?'

She takes it out and peers through it towards the horizon circling round us. 'It's all just grey fuzz in the distance and I don't like the look of these storm clouds, by the way. Not much shelter here, is there?' She takes the hoop away from her eye. 'What about your leaf?'

He draws the golden leaf out of his pocket and holds it in his palm, looking sceptical.

'I don't know what you're expecting from a leaf,' he says eventually. 'She didn't even tell me what it would do.'

'She said it would bring you back to yourself,' I remind him.

'Whatever that means!'

'Probably, the holder of the leaf needs to have a bit of faith,' Mallory says. 'Stop fighting against it and concentrate.'

He peers down at the leaf. It glints in his hand. He glances over at us with a shrug. But change is already happening – he just hasn't noticed. Behind him a slender, silver-barked tree is breaking through the hard ground, reaching for a star-filled sky. Beneath it stands the same woman who was in the visions with the Earl, but she is older, and she does not laugh. She just stares at Alberic. He frowns at our expressions and turns round.

'How tall you've grown,' she murmurs, stepping forward. 'You are Alberic.'

'Ye-es,' he says, stunned.

'My Alberic.' She walks around him, studying, her eyes hungry. 'And you think you are alone.'

'Not always.'

'But in your deepest self.'

He tilts his head to one side as she moves closer. The ground beneath her grows thick with pale green leaves.

'You never have been,' she says fiercely. 'I was always with you, Alberic. Did you never know it?'

'How would I?' he breathes, taking her in.

She stares at him. 'You have been afraid of him for too long. You have stopped listening to yourself, or to anyone else. You heard only the harsh words – you have given him your power. Take it back!'

'How?'

'Here!' she says, putting her palm against his chest. 'Can't you feel that, Alberic? Don't you know how much magic is in there? Use it! You are not only his – you are mine also! Your hair, your hands . . . Look. See it! And hear me, keep me with you. We will do this together.' She takes his hand in her other and folds it tight round the leaf. 'I am here, even if you cannot see me. I promise you, I haven't left you for a moment.'

'He's trying to find you,' he whispers. 'He wants to bring you back . . .'

'He won't be able to,' she says. 'Some things cannot be changed, even by one so great in power. What's done is done – my concern is only for you. What will you do, Alberic?'

'I wanted to bring him back home,' he says. 'I didn't know what he was doing here.'

'And if you cannot persuade him to leave this foolishness?'

'I don't know,' he says. 'They say I could bring autumn myself, but I don't know.' He says it in such a low voice, his eyes on the ground.

'Of course you can, Alberic. You've known that all along, deep down.'

'I did try. I tried back at the start of all this – it didn't work . . .'

'Because you were afraid of your father. Of being like him. You should let that go, Alberic. You'll never be like him. Can't you see that?'

She smiles, and it's Alberic's smile, wide and free, the smile we haven't seen for too long. 'Try to find him, if you must. Do what you can for him, and then do for yourself, Alberic.'

'I don't know if I can.'

'But I do,' she says, and she reaches out and lifts his chin. 'If nothing else, you can take my word for it.' She smiles again, and then a breeze skitters through the plain, and the tree curls away like a sparking wisp of smoke, and she's gone.

23

'Was that a ghost?' Mallory whispers as Alberic stares at the place where she was.

'I suppose so, in a way,' I say. 'It was the thing he needed, to bring him back to himself. The Lady's magic in the leaf allowed him to see her.'

'But was she real?'

'She seemed real to me,' I say. 'I guess the leaf works a bit like your hoop.'

Alberic is still looking at the spot where his mother stood. He lifts one hand to put it where she touched his chest, and for a moment he looks completely, utterly lost. Like a small boy abandoned just when he needed someone to be there. I take a step towards him, but words won't come, so I just stand there with Mallory, waiting. Finally he turns to us.

'OK?' Mallory asks.

He takes a deep breath and stretches to his full, majestic height. I wonder if he'll ever find a uniform to fit him, and then realize that's a really stupid thought to be having right now.

'OK,' he says. 'Let's find him, then.'

'Where did you say you thought he went last time?'

'There was a patch that felt murky, and it was hard to breathe. I kept getting turned round – I think that's where he went.'

'Well, that sounds fun,' I say.

'No it doesn't,' he says. 'But there isn't much choice, is there? We've come all this way – I'm not going to get lost here again. We just need to find him, and that will be an end to the whole thing.' His voice rings out as he says it, and a copse of tall, silver-barked trees rises in front of us, crowned in amber leaves that begin to drift towards us.

'Oh dear,' Mallory whispers as a roar shatters the air, and blows the last of the leaves from the trees. 'That's not going to be the Earl, is it? That would be too easy. Something else is there.' The ground shakes with the BOOM of footsteps, and an enormous, grey-skinned animal emerges from the trees. 'What is *that*?'

'A rhino?' I ask, taking a step back. The creature lifts its head and bellows at us, scuffing its enormous hooves against the ground.

'It's Time,' Alberic says in a flat voice as the creature begins to charge. 'Playing.'

There's no choice. No chance to do anything else. We stand together and watch the raging animal come. The ground splits as it charges, the copse of trees collapsing into a vast trench with a crash and a thunder of dust. When the creature shrieks again, the clouds break over our heads, and a furious rain begins to fall.

Time skids to a halt before us. Heat rises from its skin, and the air vibrates around its form as it collapses into the grey, hooded figure we saw when last we were here.

'Back so soon?' it demands.

'We came back for the Earl,' I say.

'You won't find him just here,' Time says.

'Then where?' Alberic asks in a steely voice.

'Have you found your power, boy?' Time asks. 'You're the only one who can find him. It was always thus, but you won't do it without your power. Your friend here found hers long ago – why has yours been hiding?' He stares at us, his eyes hungry. 'If you won't use it, you will remain here, you know. Like last time. It's fine with me. Nice to have new things in a world where nothing has been new for so long. It is all old and dusty – even my moments grow thin.' He scowls at the tumble and fall of a huge high-rise building on the horizon. 'There is nothing new in them, any more.' He turns to Alberic. 'And you stand here with all of your possibility, your future before you – why *have* you been hiding from it?'

'I'm not hiding any more,' Alberic says. 'I'm seeking.'

'The Earl is trying to change the past,' I say.

'Yes, I know. You froze me, last time you were here,' Time says, looking me up and down.

'I'm sorry. I didn't know it was possible.'

'You do seem to push against the possible,' the figure grumbles. 'All of you do, just by being here. It is that Earl's fault – he was always pushing for more. And now perhaps he *will* change everything. I can feel the thunder of his actions coming, even now. Exciting, is it not?'

'It goes against nature,' Mallory says, looking from Time to Alberic. 'Doesn't it?'

'Nature.' Time shrugs. 'Chaos is part of nature. I am the chaos part. The chance encounter, the trip and the

217

fall, the strike of lightning. There is not a plan for all things. Some of them just happen.'

'We can stop them, though.'

'You can? Then what do you need me for?'

'We don't. We came for the Earl,' Alberic says.

'Then find him, boy. If you dare . . .' And with that the figure is a funnel of smoke, a whirl of autumn leaves and stinging ice particles that sweeps around us and disappears into the distance.

'I really don't like him,' says Alberic. He watches after him for a long time, turning the leaf in his hand. And when he turns, the change in him shadows everything. The way he moves, the light in his eyes, even the way he smells. It is like iron and it threads through his veins copper-bright and sharp.

'Wow,' murmurs Mallory, grabbing my hand.

'Are we ready?' Alberic asks, his voice a rumble.

'Yes?' I manage. 'I mean, it seems like you are?'

'The thing Aurelia said about ghosts had me worried,' he says, after a moment's thought. 'I wondered if she meant my father. But of course she meant my mother. Come on, let's do this. Are you with me?'

Mallory shoots me a sideways look as he charges on, his footsteps making the earth dip and buckle. 'I mean, he knows we're the ones who *got* him here, doesn't he? *Are you with me?* Like he's the leader. Why's he gone all Hercules on us now?'

'Well, the Earl is a bit pompous,' I say. 'Maybe it's part of the power . . .'

She wrinkles her nose, and we follow him into the mist that rolls and cracks with the sound of avalanches. Alberic's footsteps get louder, the sense of him stronger. His hair glints with copper fire, his shoulders are braced and the cloaked, shadowed moments of Time begin to gather round.

'Father,' he roars, through the hordes of moments that surround us. They wink out, their faces shocked, and the way to a vast tree is suddenly clear, its crown lost high up in the clouds of an autumn storm. It's the tree from the vision, and beneath it are three figures: Alberic's mother, the version we saw in the fountain; the younger Earl; and, standing back from them, an older version. His arms are open wide, head tipped back.

'He's still making the moments repeat,' Mallory whispers as Alberic watches.

'What do we do?'

'Stop him!'

Alberic steps forward and joins the older figure of his father, unnoticed. For a moment they stand together, and Alberic watches his mother pelt his younger father with armfuls of leaves, her laughter making the air ring. And then the vision begins to falter and he steps forward.

'Alberic!' The tree disappears, and the figures before it. The Earl rounds on Alberic, his grey, creviced face wide with shock. 'What are you doing here?'

'You need to come back,' he says. 'This is no good. You're missing your season.'

'I am not only a season,' says the Earl. 'She told me that, and I forgot. Don't you want her back?'

'I do,' Alberic says. 'But it isn't real.'

'I can make it real.'

'No,' says Alberic. 'She doesn't want that.'

'How would you know?' the Earl demands. He's taller and broader than Alberic, but he's like a shadow against him, thin and grey.

'I saw her. The real version, who has been with me all along.'

'What do you mean? I haven't seen her, or even felt a whisper of her presence in all these years. Don't you think I would know if she were still here? I am an elemental, a spirit – there is nothing I don't see!'

'Oh, really,' says Alberic, reaching out and plucking something from the Earl's branch-like hair. 'You didn't see this, did you? You didn't see how you were being tricked by the Queen of May. You just strode right into this, and now the whole world is suffering, because actually you only see what you want to.'

'What?' the Earl thunders. 'What was that?'

'I planted one of the Queen's seeds on you,' Alberic says. The world seems to shift around us as he speaks. The sky is iron grey, and his skin gleams, copper leaves stirring up into the air around him.

'Why would you do such a thing?' the Earl demands, rising to his full, towering height, a roar bristling in his voice, even as he fights to keep it under control. His form is gnarled with slender branches, and now red leaves unfurl like bright daggers all about him. 'What have you done, Alberic?'

'I wanted to see if you were capable of change,' Alberic says. 'I'm not sure you are. Even here you're just trying to bend things to be the way you want them.'

'The way *I* want them! I came here for you! You need your mother. You need her humanity. I cannot *be* what you need. After last winter and everything that happened, I knew what you needed and it wasn't me.'

'We can't change any of it, though,' Alberic says. 'We lost her years ago! It's just you and me. Or it would have been, if you'd tried.'

'I did try,' the Earl says. 'I was hopeless at it. I have no patience for a small child. I have no tolerance for humanity.'

'Mother was human. You loved her. You tolerated her.'

'And look what happened!' storms the Earl. 'I lost her! Even before she died I lost her, Alberic. She'd had quite enough of me.'

'But you came back,' Alberic says in a quiet voice. 'I saw you, when you were playing with time. You came back, and you took me with you.'

'You needed me,' the Earl says in a stiff voice.

'You never stayed for long.'

'You had others to care for you. They were better suited to the task.'

Alberic takes a step towards his father, and the ground shakes beneath his feet. He towers over all of us, and the whirling copper leaves are bright explosions with sharp edges. Mallory and I step back as the Earl flounders.

'Perhaps we don't need you back,' says Alberic. 'If that's really what you think. I'll make autumn happen by myself.'

'You aren't strong enough,' the Earl says. 'All of this –' he pushes one long, slender arm through the whirling storm of leaves – 'this is just decoration, Alberic. It is very pretty, but it won't change anything.'

'No?' Alberic takes another step forward and his song breaks out around him. The earth stills, and the copse of trees behind us quietens. I feel the breath falter in my chest as fine threads of copper drive through the ground around him. The Earl is forced to stumble back. 'I think you're wrong. You made me feel small, and weak – but it was your own fear.'

'Fear?' the Earl roars.

'Yes!' Alberic roars back. 'You're so afraid you can hardly see straight, even now! What are you doing here? You should have been home months ago! The whole world is falling apart because of *you*!'

The Earl flings his arms up and a deafening tide of sorrow and rage crashes through everything. Everything but Alberic, who fights back with his own growing song. Around them, leaves spin, and the sky darkens overhead.

'Well, isn't this all very exciting?' says a child's voice, and Time is here, a small boy, golden curls bouncing. The Earl and Alberic are frozen in place, their battle suspended, and Time watches with glee. 'They're really rather wonderful, aren't they? In a completely ridiculous way.' He looks between Mallory and me with a dimpled smile as we take in shuddering breaths. 'Now. What fun shall we have? I see that your own power has been growing, little Owl . . .'

'What do you want?' I ask.

'What do I want?' Time frowns. 'Now, I don't remember the last time anybody asked me that. Isn't it kind. What do *you* want?'

'We want to go home, with the Earl and Alberic in one piece,' says Mallory.

'*Both* of them?' Time pouts. 'But it's lonely here. I like having visitors.'

'They're only visitors when they're free to come and go,' she says. 'Otherwise they're prisoners, and you've had at least one of them too long already. You have your moments, don't you?'

'Oh,' Time huffs, and gestures with one hand. A horde of shadowed figures emerges, and starts to drift off in different directions. 'I already told you I am bored of them. They are ghosts. Things that happened; some that have yet to be. They come and go in an instant – they are not friends.'

'Let them go and we will be friends,' I say with a sideways look at Mallory. I have no idea how to contend with Time, or what might happen next here. I finger the wolf at my neck and think about freezing him again. Would it be so easy? A whirl of icy wind breaks out around us as I look from Mallory to Time, an infinity of possibilities opening up around me. I see myself, alone but for a horde of sprites, stalking mountains, watching sunrise fall over snow. I see Mallory walk to school alone. Alberic, on the other side of the world from the Earl, making leaves turn to gold. My mother, sitting at the kitchen table, her eyes burning as Jack knocks at the door. I see myself in Jack's world, hunting with the wolves, skating on the lake beneath a full moon, and the bleak solitude of it pulls at me. A howl breaks the air as massive, icy footsteps begin to prowl, making the air shudder.

The pendant!

'You summon the wolves of winter into my world?' Time is fearsome and growing taller, new mountains breaking the horizon. The wolves are beside me now, their thick fur glinting silver beneath the moon. They are my wolves, here. There are five of them and their power is like a charge in my blood, and anything is possible. I rest my hand on the neck of the leader, and he growls, deep in his chest, at Time. 'Aren't they fine. Your father must be worried, little Owl. He would not let them be here so easily.'

I wince at the mention of Jack. What would it be like to have him beside me now? He'd be knowing and calm and annoying, but it would make everything feel better. I've been so angry with him, so fixated on all that was wrong when he left. Now the pain of missing him has swept in with the wolves. They are silent and still by my side, but their presence weighs more than a million of Time's fickle moments and he is afraid of them; I can see it in his eyes.

'Well?' Time demands. 'What will you do? Shall we fight?'

He is a giant now. Creviced as old rock, a beard that trails to his waist, and bright, sky-blue eyes that have seen everything.

Except me.

'If you like,' I say, swallowing down the thump of my heart, keeping my hand on the wolf just to know it's real, just to know this is all really happening. I can fight Time. I've already beaten him once.

'Your troops are most impressive,' he replies, looking at the wolves. 'But they're not a match for me, and you won't surprise me again with your little freezing trick. You are in my place. I could just make it yesterday again. Or ten minutes ago. I could set these two off on their war.' He gestures at the Earl and Alberic. 'I could take a year from your girl here.' He shrugs, looking down at Mallory. 'You are no threat to me.'

'Don't listen, Owl,' Mallory says. 'Remember what Mother Earth said.'

I frown at her, wondering what she means. Mother Earth said lots of things. She said we needed our power. And our humanity . . .

'Mother Earth?' Time laughs, and it makes the mountains shudder. 'What *has* she been saying? Some old rubbish about change, and saving the world, doubtless. It's all she ever talks about. Let me show you change. I do not only play in present and past, you know. I can show you futures. Not projections, or hopes – real futures, just awaiting the right moment. He stalks towards me, but Mallory sticks out a foot and trips him. He gives a squawk of outraged surprise before he hits the ground, shock bright on his face, and then the whole world darkens as he turns to the sky and reaches out, showing us other moments, other realities.

There is no moon, there are no stars. This is not night. This is Time. Visions play out in rushing whorls over our heads and we watch as they come. There is Alberic, taking his father's oaken staff, his face changing as he takes on the duties of the Earl. There is the Earl, locked in his own world now, away from humanity. He does not look happier for it. There is Jack, playing with Boreas in the mountains, covering an entire village in a flurry of snow that makes children laugh, even as their parents rush them into their homes.

There are the wolves of winter. They bunch their muscles and howl as they skid over ice towards their prey – shadow moments, long fingers spinning new realities even as they are run down by the wolves. And now there is a vision of Mallory, standing alone behind them. She shouts at the wolves, she shouts at *me*, but in this vision I am ice and snow and I do not hear her. I fight with the wolves. With spears of ice and tiny, stinging pellets of hail, we break the moments apart. And then it is just her.

And then I am on a dark hillside, all alone. Clouds

scud over a starry sky, and the whole of the town is lit up below me. It's infernally hot, and in the distance I see the woods ablaze. Sirens ring out, and blue lights flash, but they won't save everything.

'No!' Grief courses through me, and I fall to my knees. It isn't real. It isn't happening. Not yet. I'm in Time, on ever-shifting ground, and my friends are here. But I don't know what we're supposed to do about all those visions; they must be important. Time said they were visions of the future. The wolves snarl and Alberic and the Earl are still fighting before us. Their figures are impossibly tall and they stalk around each other, while the wind howls and dark clouds begin to spin over their heads. The Earl shoves out a narrow grey arm, wrinkled as old bark, and lightning cracks as the earth shifts beneath him. Alberic staggers back, but he doesn't falter, glaring at his father he pushes him back with a whirling tide of his own power.

'You should give this up, boy!' the Earl growls, clearly winded.

'Like you gave up on me? I won't!'

'I can't leave this place,' the Earl says, standing back, breathing hard. 'I cannot leave her, now that I have found her.'

'But it isn't really her – it's just a memory! She doesn't want you to change anything!'

'And you, boy? You don't want her back?'

Alberic stumbles back, as if hit. 'It won't happen,' he says, his eyes gleaming. 'No matter how hard you try, she's not coming back. She won't. Are you really just going to leave everything to chase impossible dreams?'

The Earl howls, and orange leaves whisk bright as knives up into the air around him, making a tornado of autumn. Alberic moves further away, shaking his head, and then his eyes catch the scenes still being played out by Time over our heads. The wolves are restless by my side. They look from me to Time now as if they don't know which side they're on.

'Mine,' I whisper, but when they look at me their eyes are like mirrors, reflecting a small, desperate girl with hair like feathers, way out of her depth.

'Did you forget?' Time whispers as the moments play out over our heads. Mallory is crying. 'Did you forget what you are fighting for? Will you fight me instead, with all the fae inside you, and risk never returning, never going back to face the reality of your broken world?'

'Humanity,' I whisper. 'Me and Alberic, we're new.

You said it yourself. In all the world, we are the new things. We are half fae, and half human. We are change that you can't control.' My voice wobbles even as I say it. All the moments Time plays with *feel* so real. 'And what you showed me isn't true,' I say, more firmly than I feel.

'Not yet.'

'So we can stop it. That's what Mother Earth meant when she spoke to me through the wooden owl, isn't it?' I say as the alpha wolf growls, hackles rising. 'That we can stop all these things happening, or at least help to, if we embrace our power. Alberic and me – we're the change. He's been blaming himself for that stupid seed, but that wasn't the change she meant. The change is who we are: human, *and* fae, and just as powerful as any of you. We need to get back to end the summer!'

The wolves are braced now, standing between me and Time, their growl reverberating through the air. He takes one step back, and they lower their backs, ready for attack.

'Yes, you do, Miss Powerful and Wise,' he says. 'I suppose I am not so averse to the idea. The world is my favourite plaything; I would miss it. But you will not have a free ride this time. Your wolves cannot win this for you. And you cannot really *win* against me here, at all. This time, you must pay.'

'What do you want?'

'A moment of your human life.' The figure shifts, and is once more the boy. His large eyes linger on the wolves for a moment, and then he flicks one hand at them with a hiss, and they are gone, unfurling like smoke, like they were never really here at all. 'You let me in, and I'll choose, just a little memory.' He smiles. 'You'll never know it's gone; you won't feel a thing!'

Mallory is still watching scenes of destruction play out over her head, and the Earl and Alberic are frozen once more, captured on opposite sides of their fight. I wonder if Time could just hold them there forever.

'And you'll let us all go? We need to land in the court.'

'Specific!' The boy laughs. 'Would you like a contract?'

'Just a promise.'

He lifts his face to mine. 'I promise,' he says, 'though I can't promise you'll be safe in the court. Time did not stand still while you played, little Owl . . .'

'Just do it, then,' I say, my chest tight. I'll never know what moment he's taken. There will be a part of me lost, forever, and I won't even know what it is. What if it's the moment Mallory and I became friends, or the moment I met Alberic? What if it's the moment Mum told me Jack Frost was my father? Or one of the moments in our kitchen, drinking tea? Suddenly they all seem too precious; I don't want to lose a thing.

But time is running out, back home. And this is the way back.

I take a deep breath and Time takes my hand. He steps closer, and my mind begins to spin. Tatters of memories, moments of colour and sound and the smell of my mother's cooking. Flashes of light, and of Jack, and Mallory, of Alberic, and the court, and Mother Earth.

An unearthly scream shatters into my mind and sends fire through my body.

We are home.

And all is not well.

24

The court is a silent glade in a silent copse of trees. The sunset sky is red, the air still so hot. The lake is quiet and the old woodland trees are wound around with vines and new, tropical blooms that are beautiful but don't belong.

I am alone, in the middle of the nothing that used to be the court. The Green Man is a silent, brooding tower, trapped and gagged by the bright green fingers of Lady Midday's endless summer.

'Mallory,' I whisper. 'Alberic?'

Silence.

'Little Owl,' comes a familiar voice as the air begins to warp with heat. I turn to see Lady Midday, her golden cloak spreading out behind her like a carpet of crushed ground. Fire sprites gather by her sides, taller, stronger than they looked before, their feet making dark patches of burned earth. She grins, as I take a step back. 'You evaded me, last time we met. I think you'll find it harder this time. I've had a good clear-out. A spring clean, you could say.'

I frown and follow her gaze to the slim birches by the side of the Green Man. They've been smothered in loops and whorls of bright new fronds, and there is the Queen of May, held tight against one of the dull trunks by ropes of green. Her pink hair is bleached to white, her skin ashen. She stares at me, but says nothing.

'You can't *do* that!' I burst.

'Who is to stop me?' Lady Midday demands, still smiling. She reaches out with one finger and trails it down the side of my face, heat scoring into my skin, and I bite my lip to stop from screaming, clapping a hand to my cheek as I pull away. 'Where is your fight, little Owl?'

I used it. I used it to get Alberic home. To get to Time to find the Earl and to get back here again. I used it to bring us all back, but not all of us are here.

'Where are your friends?' she demands as her sprites begin to move out and surround me. 'Where is your father? Do you really think you can stand alone before me, and win?'

'Win?' I manage. 'I don't know. Do you?'

'Let's try,' she says. 'Give it your best shot, little Owl.'

I put my fingers to my pendant, and think of Jack. Of what he would do in this situation. Of course he'd fight. But not with the wolves I called in Time. He'd do it with ice, thick and sharp. With snow, and frost, and quick feet. Just like I had this time last year, when winter happened and Jack came, and my magic was a bright new thing.

The sprites wink out, one by one, as ice begins to spread from my feet. It gathers pace, and I don't think, I just let it keep coming. Louder, and stronger, my blood rushing silver through my veins. Lady Midday has taken him from me. She has ruined this clearing that was full of magic and light. She has smothered the life and the magic out of everything, just because she can; she's just about ruined everything for all of us, and she won't stop without a fight. The visions Time showed me roll through my mind and I let all of my rage and fear spread through me, until the ice is a rushing lake that cracks as it reaches her feet.

Lady Midday laughs and raises one hand. A perfectly

round globe of fire smoulders there, and she holds it up before her face, and I stand on my lake of ice, knowing that if it hits me it's going to hurt a lot. My lake is becoming a puddle and the heat is melting into me.

'It was a good try,' she says, her voice gentle now. 'Little Owl. It was a brave try. But you know you have no hope against me. You don't have the power – you are just a child with tricks.'

'Would you say the same for me?' comes a rumble behind me. I don't turn. I can't take my eyes off the orange ball of flame that she's stoking, even now. I don't recognize the voice. I can hardly think straight – it's enough just to keep standing here, not melting into oblivion. My eyes are streaming, and every breath tears at my throat.

'I suppose I would,' Lady Midday says in reply. Her eyes are wide, though; whoever it is has given her a little shock. I smile, guessing who she's staring at, and then she flings the ball with an air-splitting shriek and it's too late to move.

Someone shoves me out of the way. Tall, stalking forward with a roar of his own that matches hers and takes the swell of heat out of the air. The globe of fire is flung aside, and lands in the lake, where it hisses before dwindling to nothing.

Alberic stands between me and Lady Midday. His hair is a riot of reds and golds and with every step the ground around him settles, from dusty clouds to the rich dark earth of autumn. The Lady looks at him, almost urging him on. His song thrums, sends vibrations around the clearing, and the trees spread their roots, flexing into the cool air with relief. The sky turns to smoky grey, the green vines begin to wilt.

'Little autumn,' Lady Midday says. 'Where is your father?'

'He's still working on some things,' Alberic says. 'You'll have to make do with me.'

'Very well.' She smiles. 'A battle it is, then!'

'Where's Mallory?' I whisper.

'In my house,' he says, one eye on his nemesis as the air about her begins to ripple.

'Oh!'

'We landed up there in a tangle and you were already dealing with Lady Midday, so I raced down to help . . .'

'And left her in there? She'll hate that. Where *is* the Earl?'

He ignores me, stepping forward, and all around him the air is electric. Dark, low-reaching clouds boil in the air, and funnels of hot hair snake over the ground. A bitter wind howls, and the trees bow and shake their branches, and the lake is a tidal wash of white horses, seething.

'Owl!' Mallory's voice cuts through the maelstrom, and I try to pick myself up, but the wind is so strong I can hardly move.

'Mallory?' The storm clouds gather tighter, whipping up dirt and leaves, flinging them stinging through the air. 'I can't see you!'

'. . . Green Man!' I pick out, eventually, only by closing my eyes and focusing. Alberic and the Lady are no closer, they each stand their ground, and the weather between them is terrifying. A great dark swirl of hot air and earth, of leaves, and that noxious stench of her overgrown blooms.

'. . . in Alberic's . . . but I can't open the door!' I stagger towards her voice.

'Are you OK?'

But there's only silence from her as the storm around the Lady and Alberic spreads through the clearing. The lake boils faster, more furious, until spray is falling like fine rain, carried on the bitter wind in ever expanding circles. I grab at the nearest tree, a slender birch, and pull myself up, only to be torn away and hurled across the clearing, narrowly missing the lake and falling into the rubbery leaves of some kind of cactus.

'Owl!' cries Mallory, rushing over and hauling me out. She's fought her way out of the treehouse – her clothes are torn and there are scratches on her arms and neck. 'Ouch! Does that hurt? What's going on?'

'I'm fine – how did you get out?' I ask, ignoring the stinging pain from the cactus needles.

'I had a bit of a fight,' she says. 'The Green Man thought I should stay up there out of the way, and I didn't agree. I had to bash down Alberic's door.' She winces. 'I knew you'd need my help – these plants really hate you!'

'Thank you,' I say, looking her up and down. She is battered and scratched, and her hair is standing on end, but she looks as fierce and proud as any fae queen I've ever seen. She fought to be free to help me. She *always* fights. What was that thing the Lady Midday said to me before, about humans? They'll fight, far past the point they should have given up. That is Mallory. She frowns at me now.

'What are you staring at? Are you enspelled by these horrible vines?' She drags me further away from them, the tangle of blooms shedding their nectar like poison. We both peer at the storm that hides the figures of Alberic and Lady Midday as I fold myself in next to her and give her a squeeze. 'Are you all right? What're we going to do? What's going on over there?'

'We need to get in and help,' I say, pulling away and bracing myself.

'Not much you can do in that fight,' says a familiar voice. I turn to see the Queen of May, still bound to the birch tree, but looking a lot more alert. 'That funny little autumn boy of ours, he's fighting with all his season against hers, just as his father would – and it's working!' She wrests her way free of the trapping green vine. 'Her spell is beginning to lose its power!' She moves towards us, pulling away from the last clinging tendrils, her eyes shining, pink hair flying out around her.

'You made all of this happen!' I burst. 'Look what you did, with your stupid little seed!'

'This was always going to happen,' she says with a wicked smile. 'Children don't stay small forever. Cannot be kept quiet forever. Do you not think your boy needed to find his voice?'

'But not like this!' I say, trying to see into the whirl of autumn leaves and thundering earth, flickers of lightning and tinder-hot shimmering air. 'He needs our help!'

'He has *had* your help,' she says. 'This is his part. Can't you hear him?' she asks. 'Beneath your ice, and the Lady's fire, and everything else, there it is. Autumn is not a shouting thing. It is a song that makes change happen – much like the spring, which wakes the world again.'

'It all would have happened just as normal if you'd not planted that seed and let the Earl wander off!'

'But when will you see?' she says with a sting in her voice, and the green fire of her season snapping in her eyes. 'All this had to happen. Mother Earth does nothing, curse her, without reason. Would you have left him to invisibility, to always be beneath his father's shadow? I have shown that old stick a little humility, just as I was supposed to. That is what my seeds are for. They call to the deepest part of a thing, and bring its truth to the fore. New life, new hope, new promise – and Sorbus's hope was all tied up in Alberic's mother.' She frowns. 'I had not seen that. All his bitterness, all that rage – it was all for her. He wanted only her. That is why he is not here, in the thick of it all. This isn't his fight now. He relinquished it when he left for Time.'

'What does that mean?'

'He broke the rules, Owl. He sought to manipulate Time for his own ends. He may never be allowed to return . . .'

'But it was part of the deal!' I say. 'We were all supposed to return here so that the Earl could bring autumn!'

'Who did you make a deal with?' she asks. 'With Time? He is as much of a trickster as any of us, my dear. He did not play fair.'

'Well, that is true enough.' A flash of white, through all the chaos, and Mother Earth is before us. She is small, and her hair is silver grey, wreathed with tiny star lights that wink as she moves. 'Why is this taking so long, Owl? Have I not given you all that you need?'

'I got us here, and Alberic is singing . . . and the Earl is locked in Time, still?'

She sighs. 'Some creatures take longer than others to recognize a truth. He'll be back when he is done with it.' She quirks her head to one side. 'Alberic's is a quiet song, is it not?'

'He's only just beginning.'

'And so you both are,' she says. 'You are not done, Owl. Even after this day is over and order has been restored, you will have more to do. You are the thing that stands between humanity and nature. Your power is as great as any of theirs and you will use it wisely, especially after all that you have seen. Time only showed you devastation and peril. There is much wonder out there, much that you can do to change the world. In a time of great change, you are my weapons!' She grins, and her eyes take in Mallory. 'All three of you. I could not be more proud.' Mallory's eyes light up as she watches Mother Earth fold in like smoke, to become the ghostly figure of an owl, heading to Alberic.

Mallory grips my hand in hers, gesturing towards the storm, and then I catch a flicker of Alberic's song. It smells of bonfires and carries with it a wisp of the softest cold air, something I could never make happen. Lady Midday begins to lose her golden glow. Gently, Alberic's song swells. His hair is a riot of autumn colours, and with every step the ground around him settles from dusty clouds to the rich, dark earth of autumn. The Lady looks at him, almost as if urging him on, and he steps closer, his eyes sparking with power. The song thrums, sending vibrations around the clearing, and the trees spread their roots, flexing into the cool air with relief. The sky turns to smoky grey, and the green vines begin to wilt. The horrible blooms of summer fade, and golden veins glint in the Green Man's leaves. The Lady looks at Alberic with smouldering eyes as her hordes of fae stand around her.

'You think that you will call this to an end, alone?'

'Not alone,' he says. 'Not really.'

'Where is your father?'

'Somewhere else.' Alberic shrugs. 'Does it matter?'

'I will only yield to the proper power!' she shrieks.

'You'll have to make do with me,' Alberic says. He stalks forward, taller, stranger, wilder than ever, and the forest bows before him. Leaves change in a tide, from the limp yellow-green of too much summer to red and gold and orange; they drip from the trees like falling jewels, and cover the ground. The light cuts bright and sharp through the branches, filtering in and bringing cold air to my lungs. I step away from the Queen, towards him, and frost trails in my footsteps.

'You will let her bring winter with her, before you are barely done?' demands the Lady, but it's a desperate last stand. She has already lost her lustre, and her fire sprites are nowhere to be seen. Her cloak is threadbare and dusty, her eyes dull.

'Doesn't it always seem to go that way?' asks Alberic with a grin. 'I have seen it enough times, between my father and Jack. It doesn't bother me as much as you do.' His voice thunders and the Lady steps back, but Alberic reaches for her, power bright in the air around him, his whole form outlined with the copper-bright of veins in autumn leaves. He plucks her crown from her head and the rose petals wilt as they fall, turning from pink to brown in a second. She shrieks, clutching at her golden robe as it begins to fade, as *she* begins to fade. Her sprites are smoking embers now, just the charred remains of old coal, and the Lady herself is paper thin, all the colour gone. Now she is a shifting ghost of herself, her form stretched like the gossamer webs of spiders. And then she is gone. The ground where she stood is scorched, the trees dry as paper, but she is gone.

The magic of autumn and of the fae court is instant. The lake begins to shimmer, silver flashing ripples of the moon, and the vines fall away from the trees, which begin to shift their roots restlessly beneath the dark earth. The Green Man rumbles, shaking off his shackles, and a gust blows through the court, bringing cool air and golden leaves.

I take a deep breath, and Mallory grins, rushing to Alberic. 'You did it!' she says, slapping him on the arm. He laughs, and shoves her back, and I'm about to join them when a voice heavy with a smirk rings out behind me.

'Well, that was about time,' it says, cold as steel, clear as glass.

I know before I turn around. I know, and my face betrays me with an enormous smile as Jack dances round to face me. His hair is tipped with frost, his skin covered in sharp patterns of fine ice crystals. He wears a dark cloak, and he smells of winter, and his smile matches my own.

'You came,' I say, tears spilling down my face. 'After all this time, you came as soon as you could?'

'Naturally,' he says. 'As soon as that infernal spell was broken. It is autumn, and long overdue. Soon winter, my dear!'

'I saw you fighting, back in your own world,' I say. 'Mother Earth showed me; she stopped me from coming to you. Why were you so desperate to get out?'

He looks from me to Alberic, who is talking with the Lady of the Lake, Mallory by his side, and sighs. 'I did not want you to have to do this alone. It was foolish to fight it; there is no contest against the rules of Mother Earth, but I couldn't stop myself. It was said to me last winter that change is possible, even in the world of fae. I did not understand it then. Not until the court faltered and you were here and I was trapped there. Then I felt the fear that perhaps . . . only a father might feel.'

I can't speak; my throat is suddenly tight. I take a step back from him. He is as strange and as beautiful as he ever was. Completely inhuman, utterly bewitching. My father.

'Little Owl,' he says, teasing. 'Are you overcome? I am a marvel, but I did not think to make you speechless!'

'You said father,' I whisper.

'So I did.' He grins. 'Now come. Enough of the serious — there is fun to be had!' He springs away from me towards the water, and the Lady of the Lake protests, but she's laughing as he skids across a new, thin layer of ice. I follow after him, my chest light with relief, and slide in next to Alberic and Mallory at the edge of the lake.

'You did it,' I say.

'I did.'

'Without him.'

'Yep.' He's trying to hide behind his hair, but I can see the smile on his face, and the glint in his eye. 'Only just the start, mind. Autumn for a while longer yet . . .' He looks out at Jack. 'Which might be interesting. He's not the patient sort, is he?'

'Ah no,' I say, picturing those old fights between Jack and the Earl, when ice would creep over autumn leaves, and the Earl would vent his rage upon the world. It will be different now. Even if Jack and Alberic fight, it will be different. Alberic doesn't rage in the same way; there is no bitterness about him, even after everything he's lost. 'Are you OK about it?'

'Yes,' he says. 'I forgot how much I had here, for a while – I won't forget again. I tried my best with the Earl. He'll be back one day, and hopefully better for spending time with her, even if it's all just memories.' Alberic watches as Oris appears by the Lady of the Lake, looking rather hassled. The silver water ripples as the bright-winged fairies and sprites I first saw here a year ago begin to emerge from the deepest recesses of the old copse. They flit close to us, their eyes all alight with the sight of Alberic. He is magnificent – a blaze of autumn in boy form. 'And I'm not alone,' he smiles.

'No, you're not,' I say, as Mallory links her arms through ours. We stand there for a while, watching as the massive figure of Boreas bursts into the court, beard flying, and greets Jack with a North Wind howl, scattering leaves everywhere. 'I think you're going to be pretty busy, actually.'

25

Shadows cling to dusk, and there's a bite in the air that makes my heart sing. Amber leaves drift from the trees like confetti, and even in the blue mist of dusk I can see stars overhead.

'I need to head home,' I say. 'I told Mum I'd be home by ten, after I'd saved the world . . .'

'Did you really put that on your note?' Alberic asks as Mallory laughs.

'I said I'd be honest with her,' I say. 'Will you come with me? You can stay as long as you like. I'm sorry the Earl didn't come back.'

Alberic shrugs. 'I understand better now. I didn't realize his rage was all about losing my mother, and I don't think the Lady of the Lake or the Green Man knew either – they've never known that kind of love. I thought he hated me because I reminded him of her weakness, her humanity, that was in me. I didn't see that it was just that he never stopped loving her. He was angry with the world, not me. He was grieving; he still is. I guess he always will be. He'll be back when he's stopped fighting it. Anyway –' he lifts his head and straightens his shoulders – 'I'm going to be here,' he says. 'It's my home, always has been. And it's still *mostly* here – or it will be, once Mallory's helped to fix what she broke up there.' He sighs. 'My lovely little house, all ruined.'

'I was trapped!' Mallory protests. 'I had to get away to help you both. It was an emergency. And it isn't all ruined, anyway. Just the door, and . . . I did use some of your pots for battering.'

I leave them to it, exhausted by the events of the last few days and relieved that it's come to an end, even if it didn't quite go the way we hoped it would. Just as I'm waving goodbye to the Lady of the Lake, who is accompanied by the ever-sombre Oris, Jack leaves his frosting of the trees and joins me.

'Your adventures were hard on you,' he says, bringing with him a shiver of the bitterest cold air. 'Owl?' He looks me up and down. 'Ah! You have my silver wolf! I wondered where they went galloping off to; you summoned them.' He frowns, stepping closer. 'But you're missing something, I have noticed. What is the thing that is missing?'

I hesitate. I'm tired, and I don't want any more battles, or even tricky conversations right now.

'I made a bargain with Time, for our release,' I say. 'It was nothing.'

'But not nothing,' he says.

'It was just a moment . . .'

'What moment?' he demands, stopping me and looking me right in the eye.

It's quite intense, having Jack Frost stare into you. His eyes are bright, the irises like fractured ice.

'Well, I don't know, because it's gone,' I say eventually.

He frowns, but doesn't look away.

'Jack!' I protest, dropping my gaze.

'Come,' he says. 'I see it. I'll show you.' He holds out his hand, and I frown.

It's getting dark as we reach the bridge at the centre of town. Fairy lights glitter, outlining it against the sky.

'Wait here,' says Jack. 'And begin across it, in a moment.'

I wrap my fingers round the handrail as I start on to it, and frost immediately spills from my grip, a fine veil of it that spreads over the railing. In the dim light, my skin is almost blue, and the ice beneath my feet winks. There's a soft booming sound, and the whole bridge seems to vibrate. I look across to the other side and there he is, my father, coming on a tide of ice that sweeps out in a great swell, making jagged ridges to either side of us, the centre walkway of the bridge smooth as an ice rink, every upright line covered in a thick fur of frost. The whole thing glows and, coming towards me, Jack Frost is a vision. The air around him blurs with a thousand little shards of ice. His dark hair is tipped with frost, and his grin is wicked sharp.

'What are you doing?' I ask.

'This is the moment,' he says. 'Not perhaps the exactitude of it, but as close as I can bring you. This is the moment Time took. The moment you first saw me.'

'I . . . I remember running away from the bridge . . .' I frown. My chest falters; there is a gap there, a dark place that hurts when I poke at it.

'Yes,' he says. 'I did not know you then. I frightened you. Do I still, little Owl?' He raises his palms, and pulls pillars of twisted ice from the ground.

I tilt my head to one side, considering. Then I spread my own hands and the pillars I make are more slender, but they are every bit as beautiful, and every bit as magical as his.

'Not so much.' I grin. And we skate down the bridge, faster, and faster, blizzards of snow breaking out in the air between us, and in that moment something inside me settles. Something that *was* afraid of him. Afraid of being like him.

I *am* like him. And I'm not.

I'm me.

26

Later, exhausted and buzzing from adventure, I head back into town and Jack walks with me. The ice on the bridge melts as soon as we step away from it; autumn is new and the air is still warm. Jack is oddly quiet beside me and I keep expecting him to disappear, but he doesn't. The gap in my memory still hurts when I think of it, but knowing what it is that I have lost helps, and so does my new image of winter across the bridge. Of Jack and I, ice cold and free. Ready to fight for our season.

'Isolde will be home?' he asks eventually, as we round the corner to our flat.

I look at my watch. 'Probably.' I wince. 'I'm supposed to have stayed in this evening.'

'I should come with you and explain a little.'

I stop in the street, and stare at him. The ground turns white beneath my feet, and my hair prickles with frost.

'Did you get locked in your world with a *parenting manual*?'

His eyes glitter. 'What is one of those?'

'Never mind. You really want to come back with me?'

'For a moment,' he says with a shrug. 'She is not so terrifying, is she?'

'Not ordinarily,' I say.

'Then lead the way, little Owl,' he says, gesturing ahead of us with a great spill of frost.

The front door has never been so heavy, or so difficult to open. The stairs have never been so slippery. The door to the flat has never squeaked so loud. With every step I take, my heart thumps in my ears.

It'll be fine. I know it'll be fine. She'll be delighted, and even if they don't get on, that won't be the end of the world. It just feels weird. I think about Mallory and everything she's been through with her parents separating and I wonder if it feels a bit like this. Like everything's shifted and the ground beneath your feet isn't firm any more. You know it will be again, one day, but right now it just feels like falling.

'Owl?' Jack loiters on the steps. I turn to see that the whole place looks like an ice cave. Banisters are covered in inches of snow, icicles hang from the ceiling and beads of frost are scattered over all the whitewashed walls; he's been building it on his way here. He's as nervous as I am. 'This is your world,' he says. 'If you don't want me here . . .'

But I do, I realize, staring at him. I do at least want them to *meet*.

'What if it goes wrong?' I whisper.

'It won't,' he says after a moment, his eyes brightening. 'It can't go wrong – there is no pattern to be right or wrong with! It is *new*.'

'Wait here a minute, then,' I say, making him stay on the landing as I head in. The flat looks the same. Same white walls, same wooden floor. Same smudges and blotches of paint on the kitchen table. The fridge is still groaning. My mother trips down the stairs from her studio and she looks just the same. Her dark eyes glow, her hair is bundled on to her head. There are little flecks of grey in it and they spark in the light.

'Owl! I said you should be here when I get home! What is it? What's wrong?'

'Nothing's wrong,' I say, through dry lips. 'Um. There was a bit of an adventure, but it worked out fine . . .'

'I thought so!' she crows, coming closer, putting her arms around me. 'I felt the stirrings of the first frost on my way home and I *knew* something had been going on!' She steps back, and studies me. 'Are you all right? You look pale.'

'I'm OK,' I say. 'I'm going to go out and meet Mallory and Alberic, if you don't mind. I just wanted to check in first.'

'Have you eaten? I made some aubergine muffins – you can take some with you . . .' She pulls me into the kitchen and propels me to a chair, and starts fetching things. I watch for a while, trying to find the right words. Any words at all, really.

And then she turns, and frowns.

'Owl? You're too quiet. What is it?'

'I brought Jack . . .'

The End

Acknowledgements

My first and greatest thanks are to you, dear reader. Without you this book would not exist, and I have so enjoyed returning to Owl's world. I hope that I have done her justice, and that you have enjoyed it too.

Thank you to all the teachers, reviewers, bloggers and authors who have taken the time to read my books and share your passion with others, I am in awe of you all.

Thanks, then, to my wonderful editor Lucy Pearse, and to all at Macmillan, for continuing to put your faith in me and my stories. I will never quite believe it, but to the extent that I do, I am so grateful. Thank you to Kat, Jo, Amber, Sabina, and to Vron, and to Rachel Vale and Helen Crawford-White for these gorgeous covers.

Thank you to my agent, Amber Caraveo, whose passion is chandelier-bright, even on the darkest days. Thank you to my fellow Skylarkers, for conversations late at night and early in the morning, about everything and especially about goats. Thanks to Lu, and Aviva, and Caroline. Thank you, Lee, and thanks to Theia, Aubrey and Sasha. And a special thanks to David Goldstein.

It has been a year none of us will ever forget, and I am privileged to have shared it with you all.

Turn the page and discover where it all began,
in an exclusive extract from the spellbinding
A Girl Called Owl

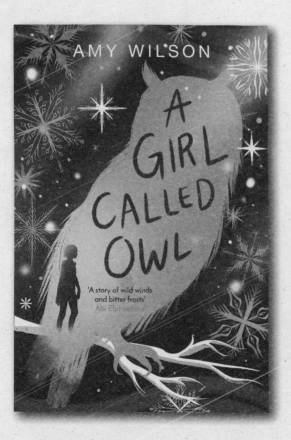

'A story of wild winds and bitter frosts'
Abi Elphinstone

1

When you have a kid, don't call it something stupid.

Don't call it Apple, or Pear, or Mung Bean.

Don't call it Owl.

This advice is a bit late for me. Because she did. She did call me Owl. Thirteen years ago she looked down at a tiny little baby – me – and decided that Owl would be a good way to go.

I guess she didn't know then that I would grow up to have white-blonde hair that flicks around my face like feathers, no matter what I do with it. That my eyes would turn from baby blue to the palest brown, almost yellow; that my nose would be on the beaky side.

She should have seen that last one coming, though; I inherited it from her.

I like owls. I think they're beautiful. But you know,

my head doesn't rotate 360 degrees. I can't fly. I don't hunt at night.

All these are questions the other kids have asked me, over the years. Mum laughs when I tell her.

'See!' she cries, looking up from whatever she's doing, a glint in her dark eyes. 'Already you stand out from the crowd. Already you are different. Isn't it a wonderful thing?'

She's beautiful, my mum. Not in a subjective way, like she's my mum therefore she must be beautiful. She's actually beautiful. She has these big dark eyes, masses of dark hair and when she smiles, when she laughs, it's very difficult not to join in.

I do try my very best not to join in.

Her name is Isolde. She wears lots of bright colours, and tinkling bangles on her wrists. She smells of warm things: vanilla, cinnamon, oranges and blackcurrants, and something deeper that's just her, I guess.

My friends love her.

Which is annoying.

'Owl McBride!'

I look up from my desk. Mr Leonard is perched on the edge of his table, his ankles crossed in front of him.

His hands rest on the table, one finger tap-tapping against it. There's a diagram on the board behind him but it's all squiggles to me.

'Are you concentrating?'

'Yes, sir.'

'On the lesson, I mean, as opposed to your doodling?'

I blush as a roll of laughter goes around the room.

'Yes, sir. Sorry, sir.'

'That's all right. If you can tell me what *pi* is.'

Clearly it'd be a bad idea to tell him it's something I eat with my chips. His eyebrows are just daring me to do it. They look like black marker pen stripes, drawn too high on his forehead, trying to hide beneath his shaggy dark hair.

'It's where the circle has a diameter and the circumference is . . . when you calculate it . . . that's *pi*.'

I smile hopefully, but Mr Leonard drops his head and sighs.

'I suppose,' he says, standing up and walking to the board. 'I suppose I should just be happy that you know the right words, even if you've no idea what to do with them.'

He starts jabbing at the board with a blue marker, making more squiggles. I copy them down in my book. The rest of the class does the same.

Mallory, next to me, is still laughing.

'Shh!' I hiss at her, my pen moving across the paper, making alien mathematical shapes I've no use for.

It was an owl. The doodle in my maths book. I draw them, over and over. Little ones, big ones, owls with crazy whirly eyes, owls swooping from the sky. They're in all the borders of my lined schoolbooks. They're on Post-it notes around my bedroom. I have sketches of them, paintings, even little clay figures.

I'm not saying they're good. Actually, if you walked into my bedroom you'd probably run back out again screaming. They're a bit intense.

Mum loves them. *Loves* them. She thinks it's me expressing myself.

Drawing myself, over and over again.

Mallory just rolls her eyes when she sees a new one now. She bought me a card with a puffin on it for my birthday a couple of weeks ago.

'Maybe a change?' she wrote inside. 'Now that you're thirteen?'

But I'm not *called* Puffin.

And there has to be a reason.

A reason Mum called me Owl.

2

Clearly I must have a father somewhere. Everybody has one, after all.

But Mum won't tell me who he is. There are no photos, no certificates with his name on. Nothing. And whenever I ask her she goes all misty-eyed and tells me he was a beautiful man, who left her a beautiful gift. She wanders off to see him in her imagination and leaves me behind, in the kitchen, for example, while dinner starts to burn.

When I was younger, she would tell me fairy tales about how they met in one of the magical wintry lands from her old storybook, and I loved them, because it *was* magical, and I was just a kid. But I got older, and it started to annoy me, because I wasn't a kid any more, and I wanted real answers.

So she stopped with the stories and got vague instead. And that's the source of most of our arguments.

That and the Owl thing.

It's nearly impossible to have a satisfying argument with my mum. She watches seriously while you make your initial point. She considers, nodding, and then tells you something completely pointless.

'Dear sweet child,' she says now, deflecting my latest attempt to ask about fatherly things as I untangle myself from my scarf after school. 'Some things are not supposed to wear labels, or names. Some things remain a mystery, however hard we butt up against them . . .' She smiles, pouring jasmine tea into two tiny china cups and pushes one along the kitchen counter to me.

'So you don't know who he is, then?'

'Oh, I know him,' she says, picking up her own cup and looking down at the steaming amber liquid. 'I've told you about him, Owl, you just never believed me . . .'

'Well if you know him, he must have a name,' I say. 'And you can give it to me. Can't you?'

She takes a sip.

'Owl, drink!' she says, when she's finished. 'It's only good when it's hot.'

I take a sip.

'I have nothing to give you except this moment,' she says then. 'That is all there is. You and I, in this kitchen, drinking our tea.'

The china cups have jade green dragons inside them, eternally chasing their tails around the white background, breathing fire at themselves.

Sometimes I feel a bit like those dragons.

'Who needs a dad, anyway?' sighs Mallory on the phone later, when I tell her of my latest failed attempt.

That's easy for her to say. Hers is probably outside cleaning the car right now. I look out of the window, as if mine might just be there, looking for me, waiting for me to notice him. Brittle autumn leaves fall from the trees on the street and a little shiver runs down my spine; mid-November, and winter is here. Soon there will be frost and ice sweeping over the rooftops, curling down trees, making the grey pavements sparkle. The thought makes my skin itch, makes me impatient. The need to know where I come from is almost overwhelming.

'. . . and flipping annoying,' Mallory's voice cuts in. 'Honestly, you don't need a dad, Owl.'

'I do,' I tell her firmly. 'At least his name . . .'

'You are a bit fixated on names.'

'And why do you think that is?'

'Mallory isn't all that, you know. It's the name of an Enid Blyton school, for goodness sake.'

That's true enough. But it's better than Owl.

We spend the rest of the conversation talking about Justin. Mallory talks a lot about Justin. She's convinced they're soulmates, even though he's going out with Daisy.

'Double English tomorrow,' she says as we say our goodbyes. 'A whole hour and a half of English!'

Which means sharing a class with Justin. Which means they'll compete with each other every time a question is asked, and try to answer it in the most complicated, literary way possible, and I just have to sit there and watch it all and feel a bit stupid. I usually have a couple of new owls by the time I come out of English lessons.

I chuck the phone on to my bed with a huff and go to the window, muttering to the carved owl on the bedpost about how boys complicate everything. As I watch, half distracted, something moves between the trees outside the flat, something lean and hunched, with spidery limbs; something so alien, so out of place, that my skin tightens with fear before I've even worked out what it is. I lean closer to get a better look, my breath misting the glass, but all I can see is shadows.

I have a good imagination. It was probably just a fox. I pull the curtains with a sharp tug and tell myself off for being such a kid.

About the legends Mum used to tell me. She hasn't got that old book out for years now, and I sort of miss it. I'd never admit it, but when I struggle to get to sleep sometimes I imagine the stories were true, and my father really is from some great fantasy land. I remember the way her voice changed as she told me of those strange places; the way her eyes glazed as she spoke of fairies and sprites, talking trees and fearsome queens. Sometimes it was a little scary – as if I'd lost her to that other world.

*I*t was ever winter there. The deepest, coldest, the bluest winter; the winter of the world. The sky changed as day turned to night and night to day once more but the sun was a cold white disc in the sky, and the moon shone brighter against the darkness but still there was no heat about it.

Her ears screamed with the dead silence in the air.

Her chest burned to breathe against the bitter of the wind.

He found her, in the clearing between the trees that towered out in every direction: black with bark and white with frost. He found her by the plume of her breath, by the snap of frozen twigs beneath her boots as she turned and turned and turned again, waiting for something to become familiar.

Nothing was familiar.

He was blue-white as if he'd never seen the summertime. His eyes were mirrors in the dawn and his dark hair was tipped with the frost of the land. When he reached out his hand she thought it would be like ice.

It was not.

He gestured back the way he'd come and his grip tightened. She breathed in and prepared to launch her questions at him, but even as her lips gathered he shook his head and put a finger to her mouth.

'Not here, not now.'

'But why am I here and what is this place and where is home and where am I and who are you?'

He considered her and took his hands away and she was colder than she had ever been and clung to herself, but he was quick to unclasp his robe and sweep it over her shoulders.

Once more he took her hand.

'Now?'

'Now we run.'

The cloak he'd drawn around her was charcoal grey and heavy. It was the rough-smooth of new wool and though the plain was freezing and the wind howled in her ears she was not cold.

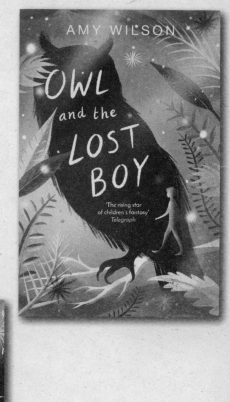

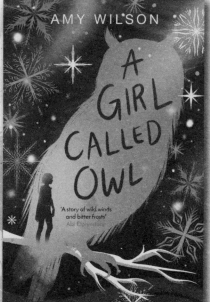

About the Author

Amy Wilson has a background in journalism and lives in Bristol with her young family. She is a graduate of the Bath Spa MA in Creative Writing. *A Girl Called Owl* was longlisted for the Branford Boase Award, nominated for the Carnegie Medal and shortlisted for a number of regional awards. Her middle-grade novels include *A Girl Called Owl*, *Owl and the Lost Boy*, *Snowglobe*, *Shadows of Winterspell* and *A Far Away Magic*.